FLUFFY
STRIKES BACK

A P.U.R.S.T. ADVENTURE

KIDS CAN PRESS

TO ROD, GLORIA AND SHANE, MY OTHER FAMILY

Kids Can Press acknowledges the financial support of the Government of Ontario, through the Ontario Media Development Corporation's Ontario Book Initiative; the Ontario Arts Council; the Canada Council for the Arts; and the Government of Canada, through the CBF, for our publishing activity.

Published in Canada by
Kids Can Press Ltd.
25 Dockside Drive
Toronto, ON M5A 0B5

Published in the U.S. by
Kids Can Press Ltd.
2250 Military Road
Tonawanda, NY 14150

www.kidscanpress.com

The artwork in this book was rendered in Photoshop, under constant threat of alien attack.
The text is set in Fontoon.

Edited by Yasemin Uçar
Designed by Julia Naimska

The hardcover edition of this book is smyth sewn casebound.
The paperback edition of this book is limp sewn with a drawn-on cover.
Manufactured in Shenzhen, China, in 10/2015 by C & C Offset

CM 16 0 9 8 7 6 5 4 3 2 1

Library and Archives Canada Cataloguing in Publication

Spires, Ashley, 1978–, author, illustrator
        Fluffy strikes back / written and illustrated by Ashley Spires.
  (A P.U.R.S.T. adventure)
ISBN 978-1-77138-127-7 (bound) — ISBN 978-1-77138-133-8 (pbk.)
        I. Title.
PS8637.P57F58 2016   jC813'.6   C2015-903113-3

Kids Can Press is a *Corus*™ Entertainment company

SOME NAMES HAVE BEEN CHANGED
TO PROTECT THE IDENTITIES OF
PETS WHO APPEAR IN THIS BOOK.
ANY SIMILARITIES TO ACTUAL
EVENTS ARE PROBABLY BECAUSE
THIS ACTUALLY HAPPENED.

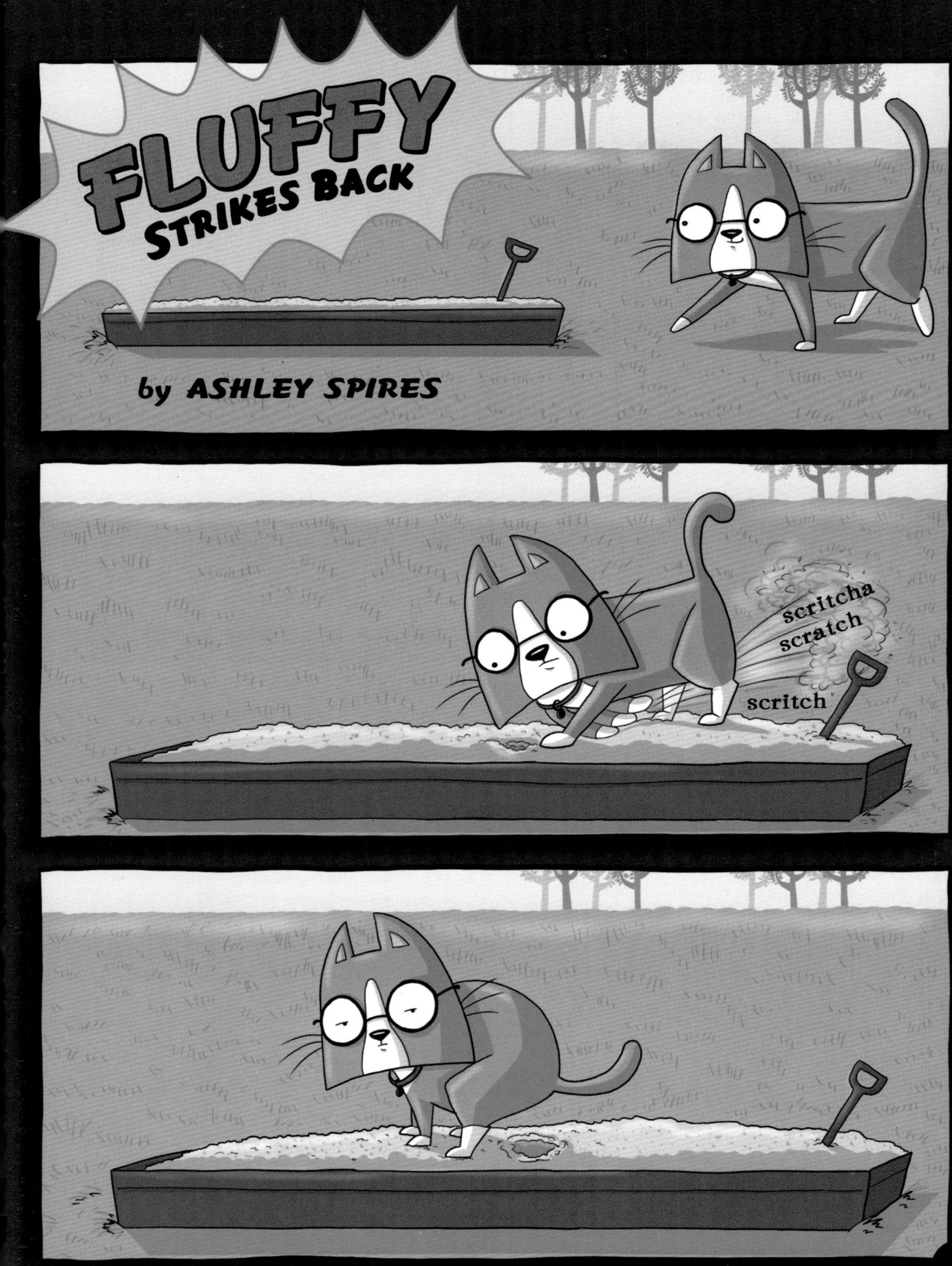

FLUFFY STRIKES BACK
by ASHLEY SPIRES
scritcha
scratch
scritch

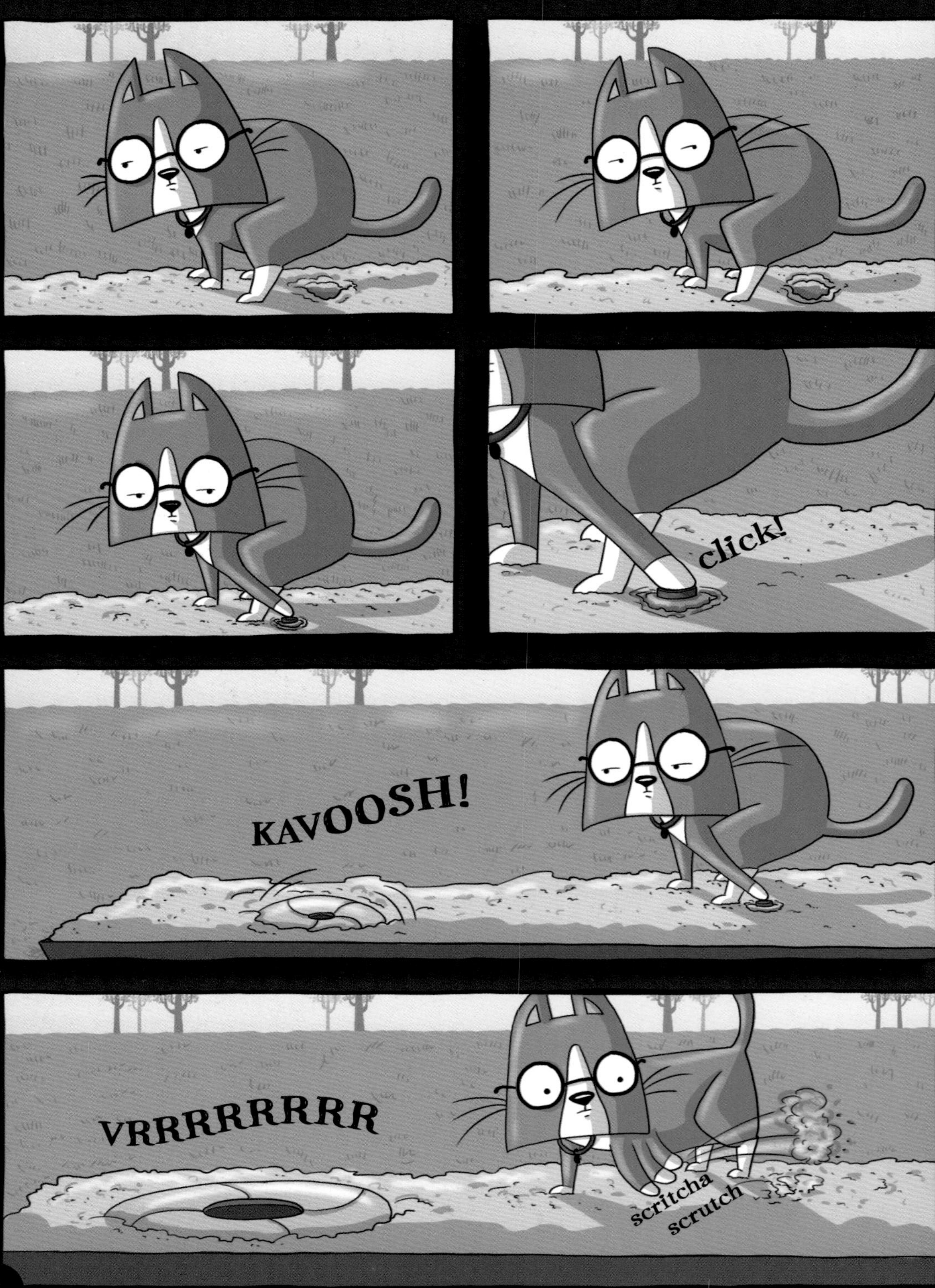
click!
KAVOOSH!
VRRRRRRRRR
scritcha
scrutch

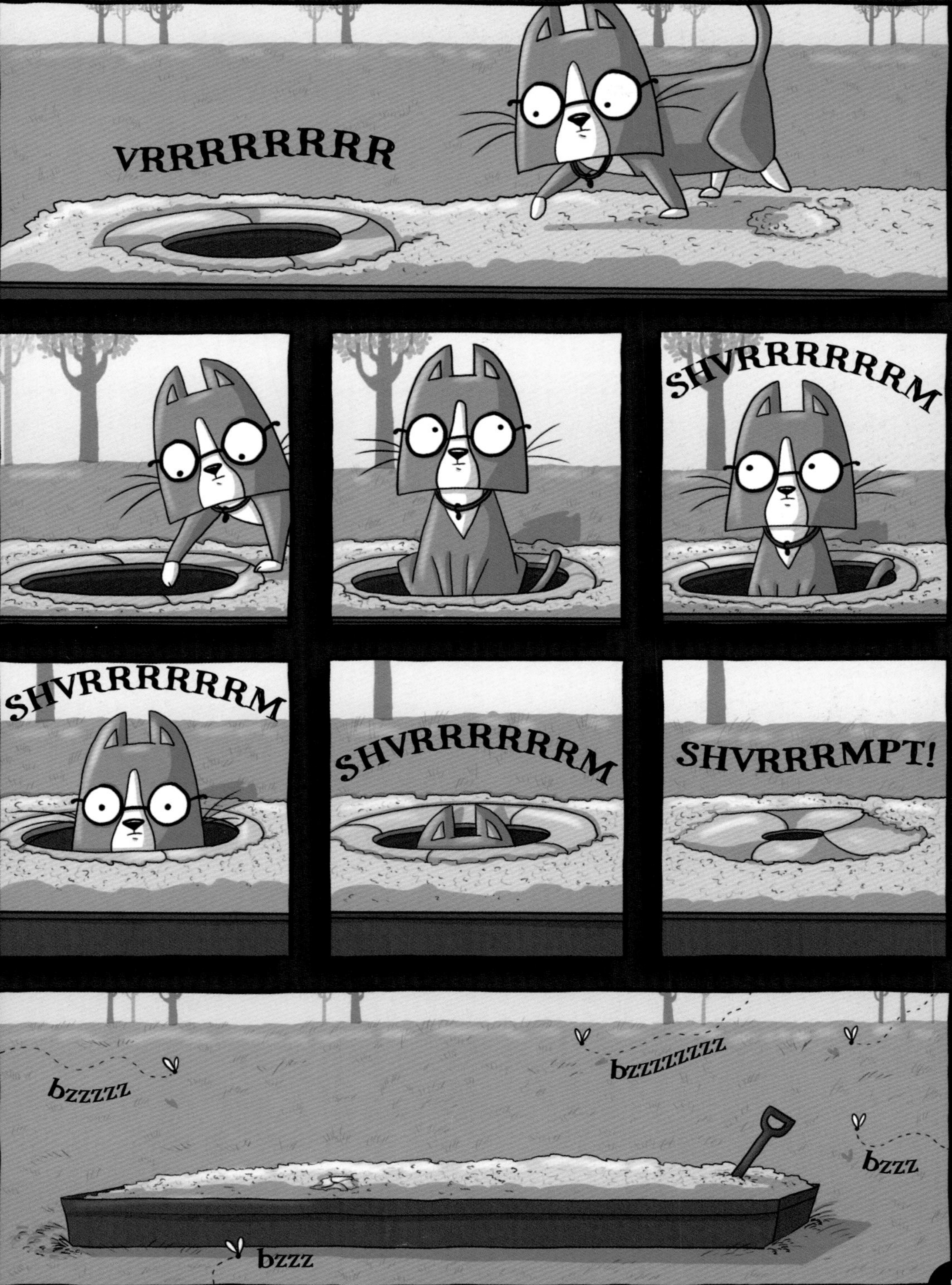
VRRRRRRRR
SHVRRRRRRRM
SHVRRRRRRRM
SHVRRRRRRRM
SHVRRRMPT!
bzzzzz
bzzzzzzz
bzzz
bzzz

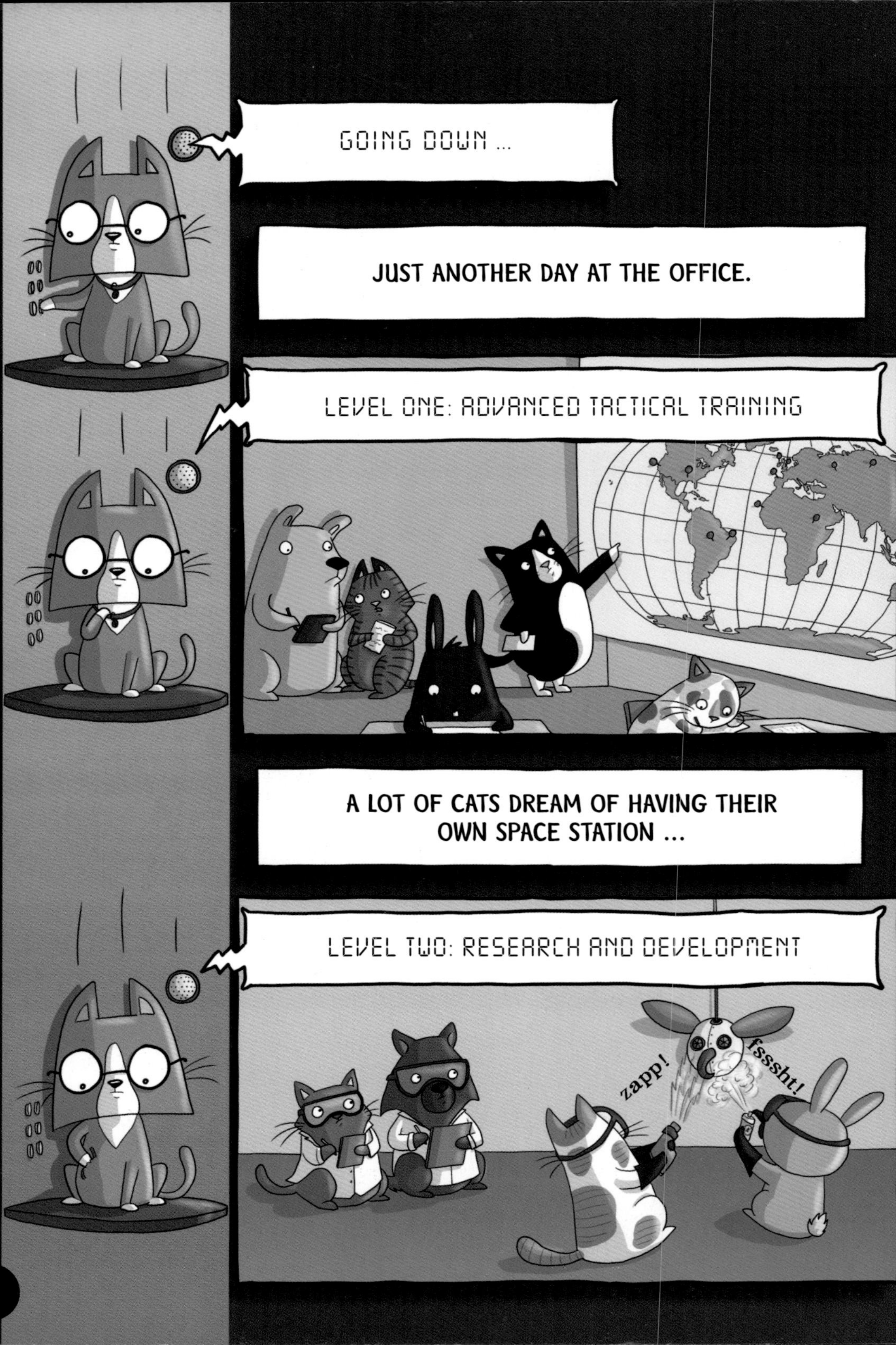
GOING DOWN ...
JUST ANOTHER DAY AT THE OFFICE.
LEVEL ONE: ADVANCED TACTICAL TRAINING
A LOT OF CATS DREAM OF HAVING THEIR OWN SPACE STATION ...
LEVEL TWO: RESEARCH AND DEVELOPMENT
zapp!
fssshht!

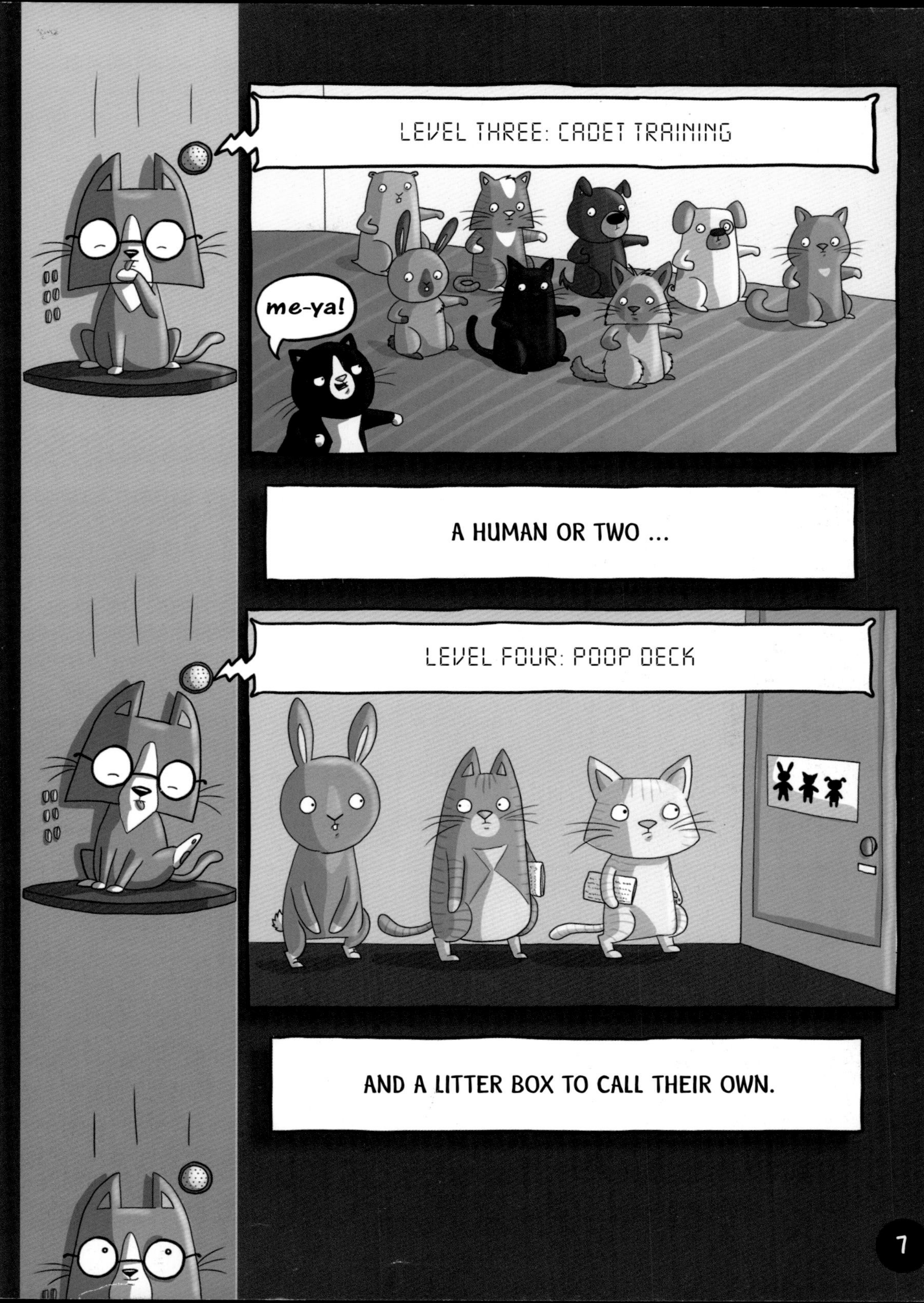
LEVEL THREE: CADET TRAINING
me-ya!
A HUMAN OR TWO ...
LEVEL FOUR: POOP DECK
AND A LITTER BOX TO CALL THEIR OWN.

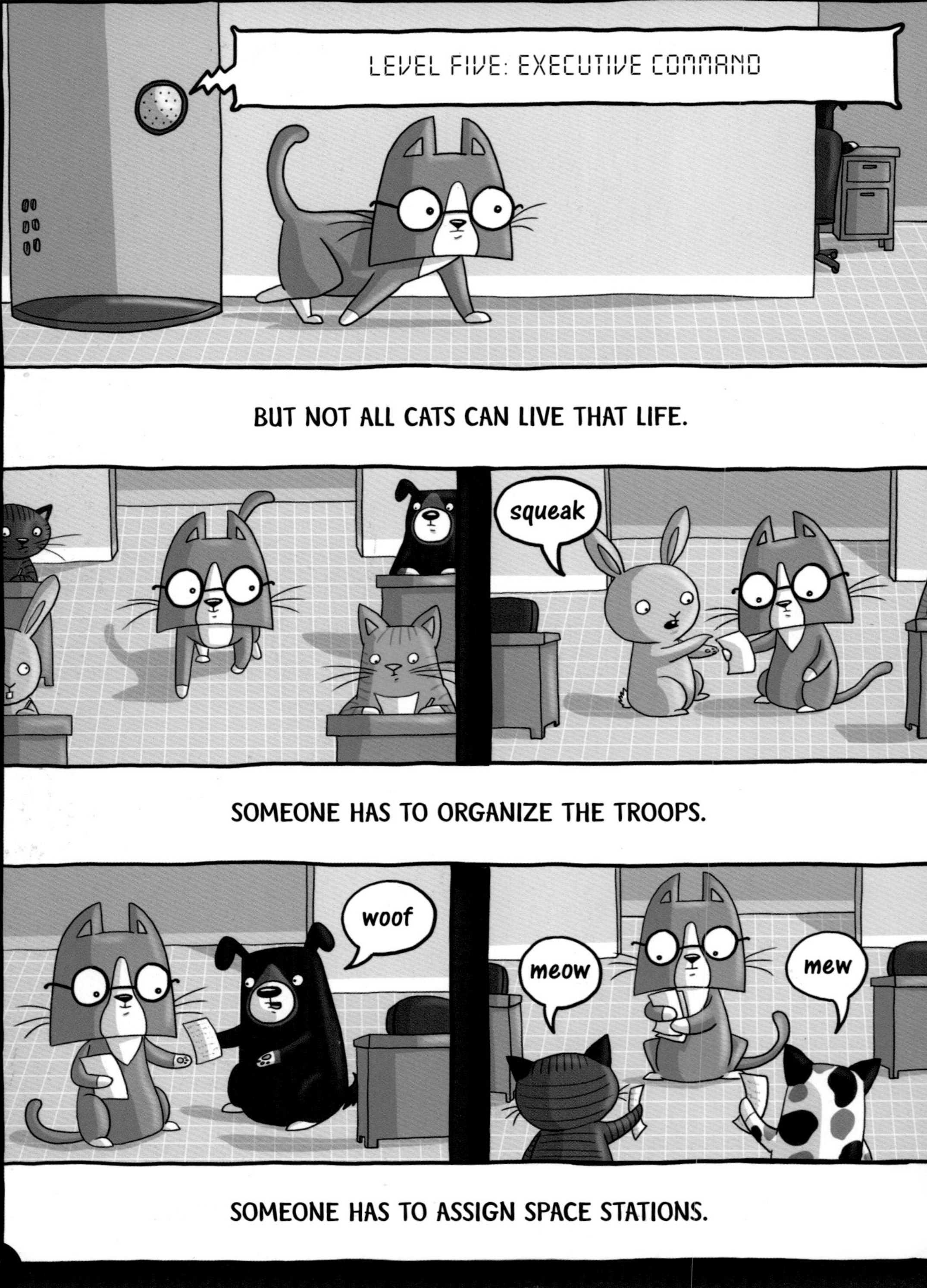
LEVEL FIVE: EXECUTIVE COMMAND
BUT NOT ALL CATS CAN LIVE THAT LIFE.
squeak
SOMEONE HAS TO ORGANIZE THE TROOPS.
woof
meow
mew
SOMEONE HAS TO ASSIGN SPACE STATIONS.

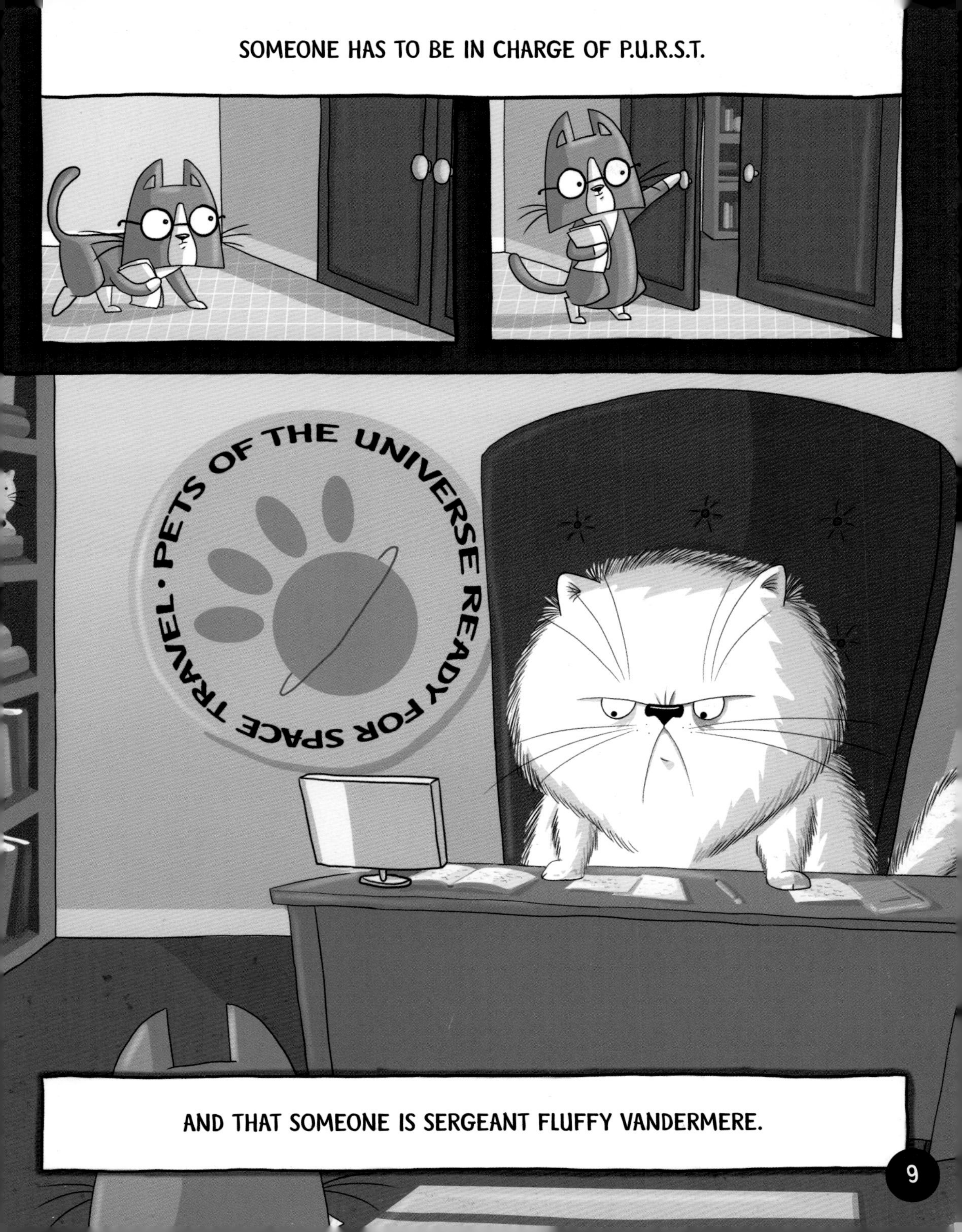
SOMEONE HAS TO BE IN CHARGE OF P.U.R.S.T.
PETS OF THE UNIVERSE READY FOR SPACE TRAVEL
AND THAT SOMEONE IS SERGEANT FLUFFY VANDERMERE.

AS THE LEADER OF P.U.R.S.T. ...

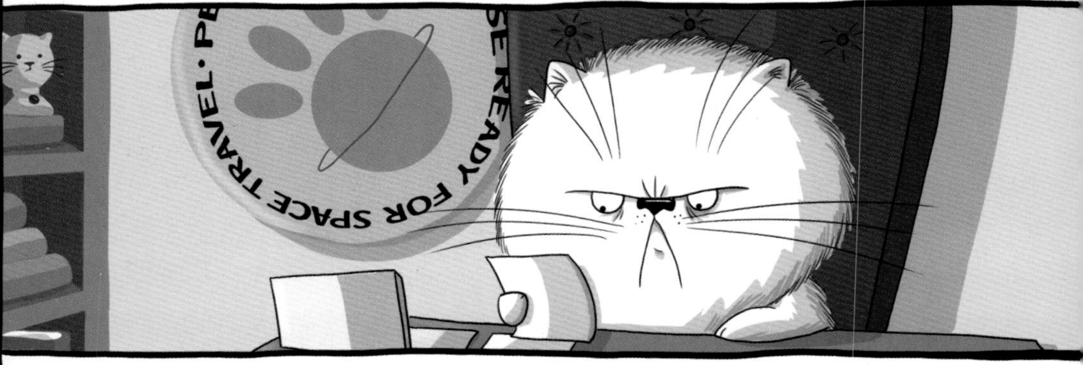

READY FOR SPACE TRAVEL

FLUFFY CAN'T HAVE ANY DISTRACTIONS.

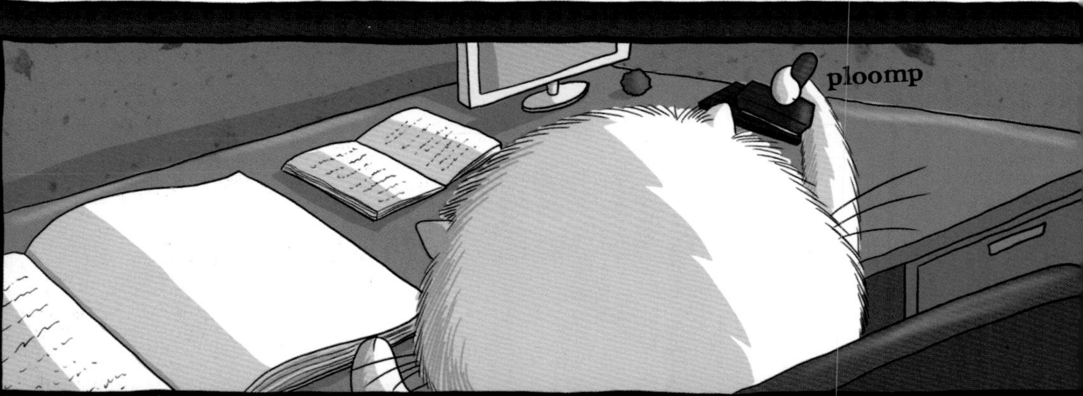

ploomp

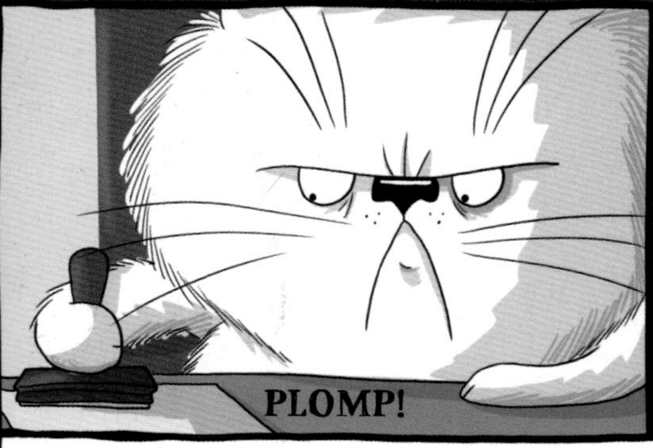

PLOMP!

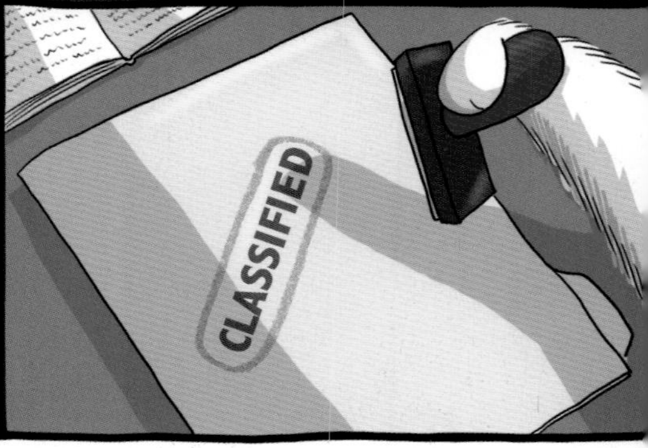

CLASSIFIED

HIS JOB IS TO PROTECT THE WORLD FROM ALIEN DOMINATION.

THE **WHOLE PLANET** IS FLUFFY'S SPACE STATION.

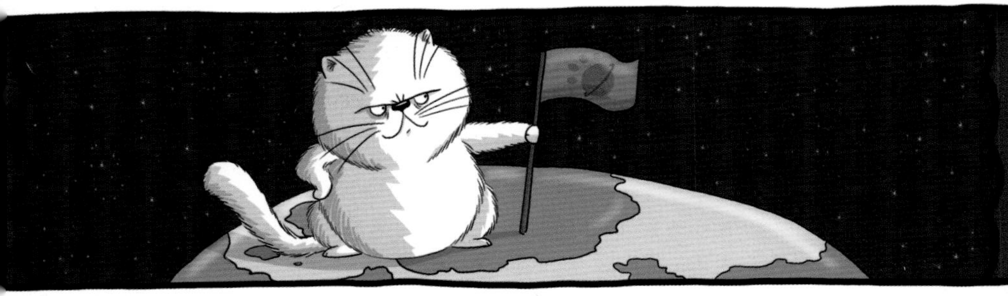

ALL THE PEOPLE IN THE WORLD ARE **HIS** HUMANS.

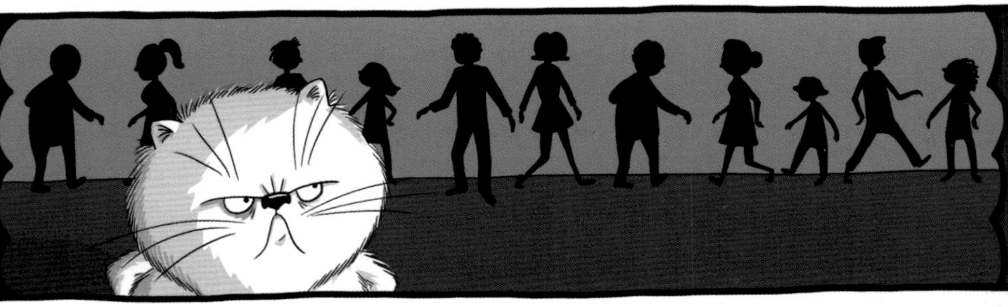

AND EVERY SPACE PET OUT THERE IS **HIS** RESPONSIBILITY.

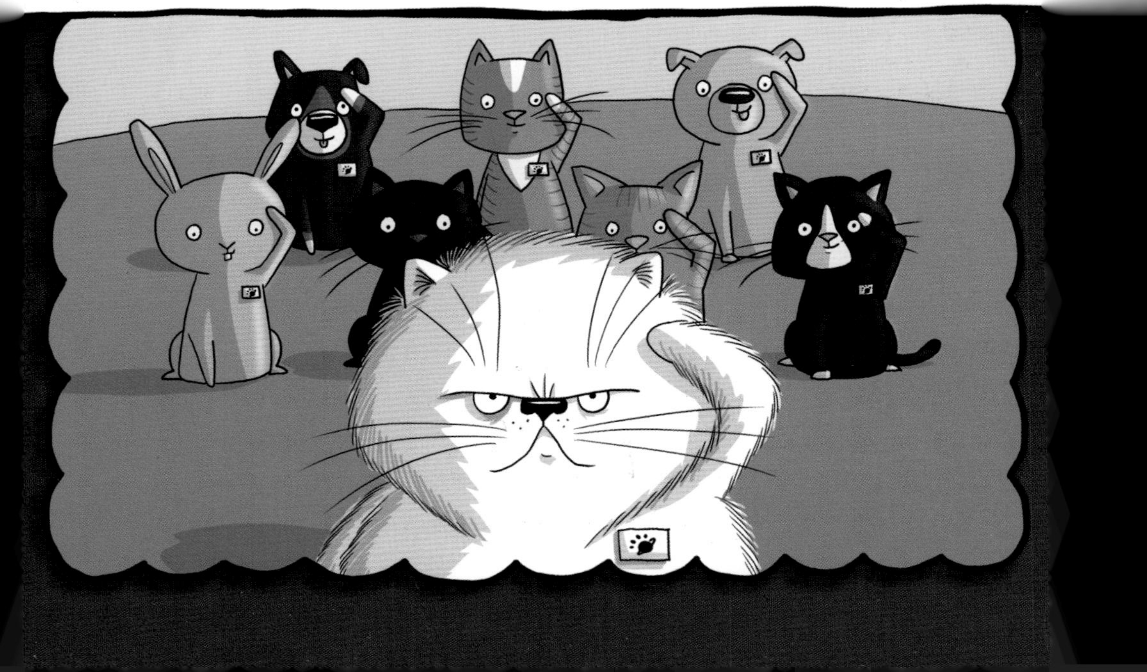

OF COURSE, EVERY GOOD LEADER NEEDS A RIGHT-HAND CAT ...

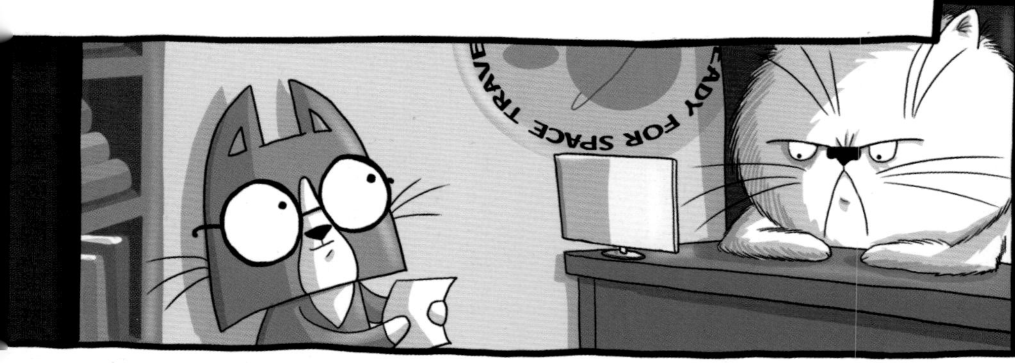
EADY FOR SPACE TRAVE

AND THAT'S WHERE CLICK COMES IN. SHE'S HIS EYES AND EARS.

SHE MONITORS ALL OF P.U.R.S.T. BUSINESS ...

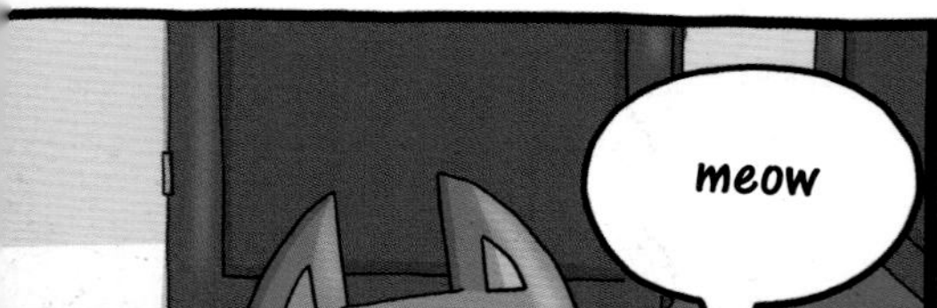
meow

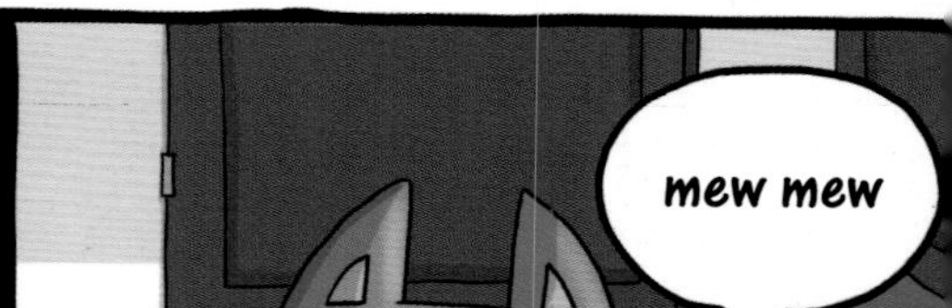
mew mew

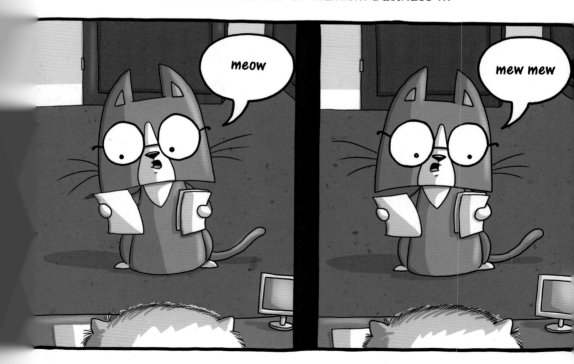

AND RELAYS ALL IMPORTANT INFORMATION TO THE SERGEANT.

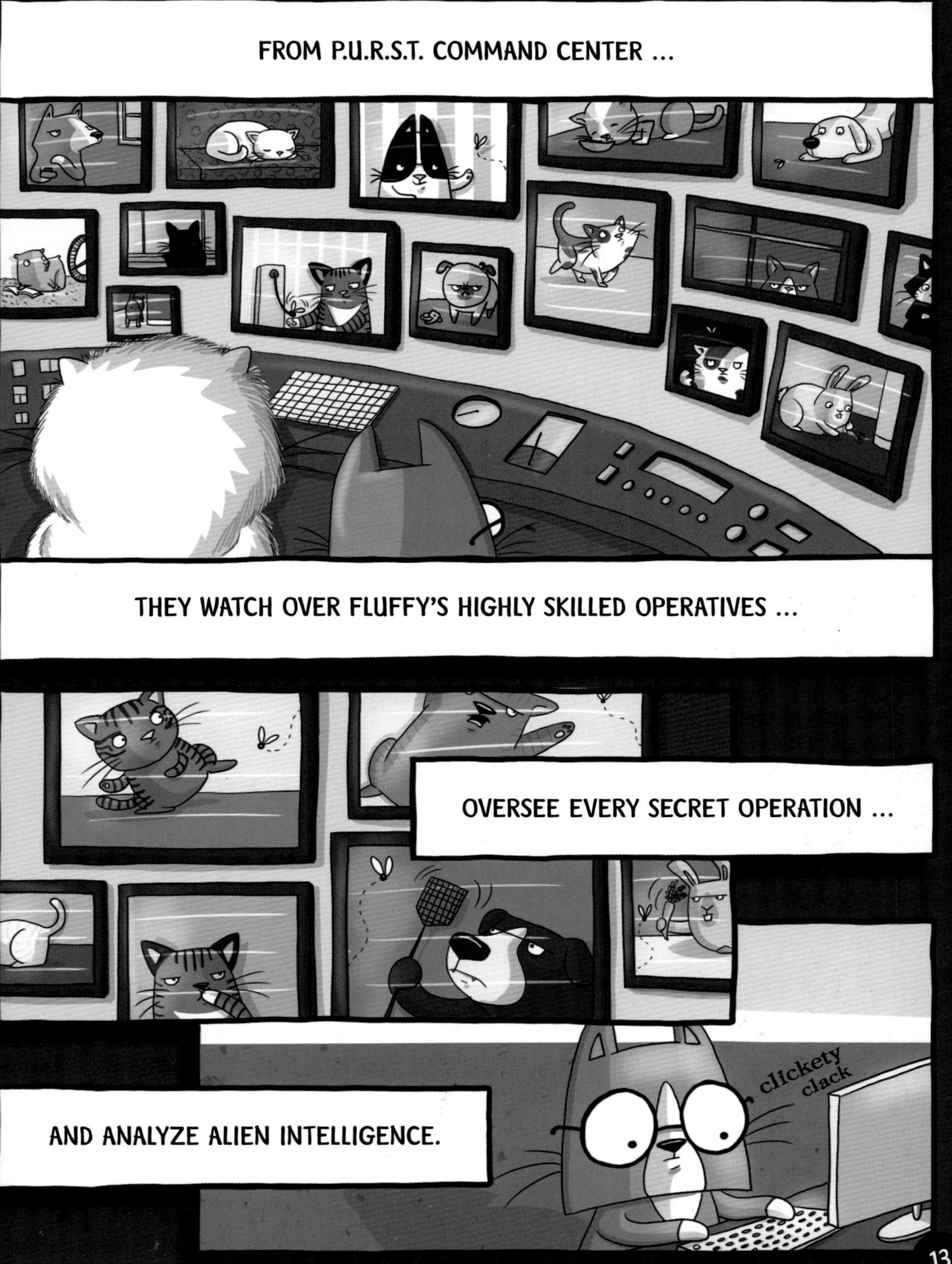
FROM P.U.R.S.T. COMMAND CENTER ...
THEY WATCH OVER FLUFFY'S HIGHLY SKILLED OPERATIVES ...
OVERSEE EVERY SECRET OPERATION ...
AND ANALYZE ALIEN INTELLIGENCE.
clickety clack

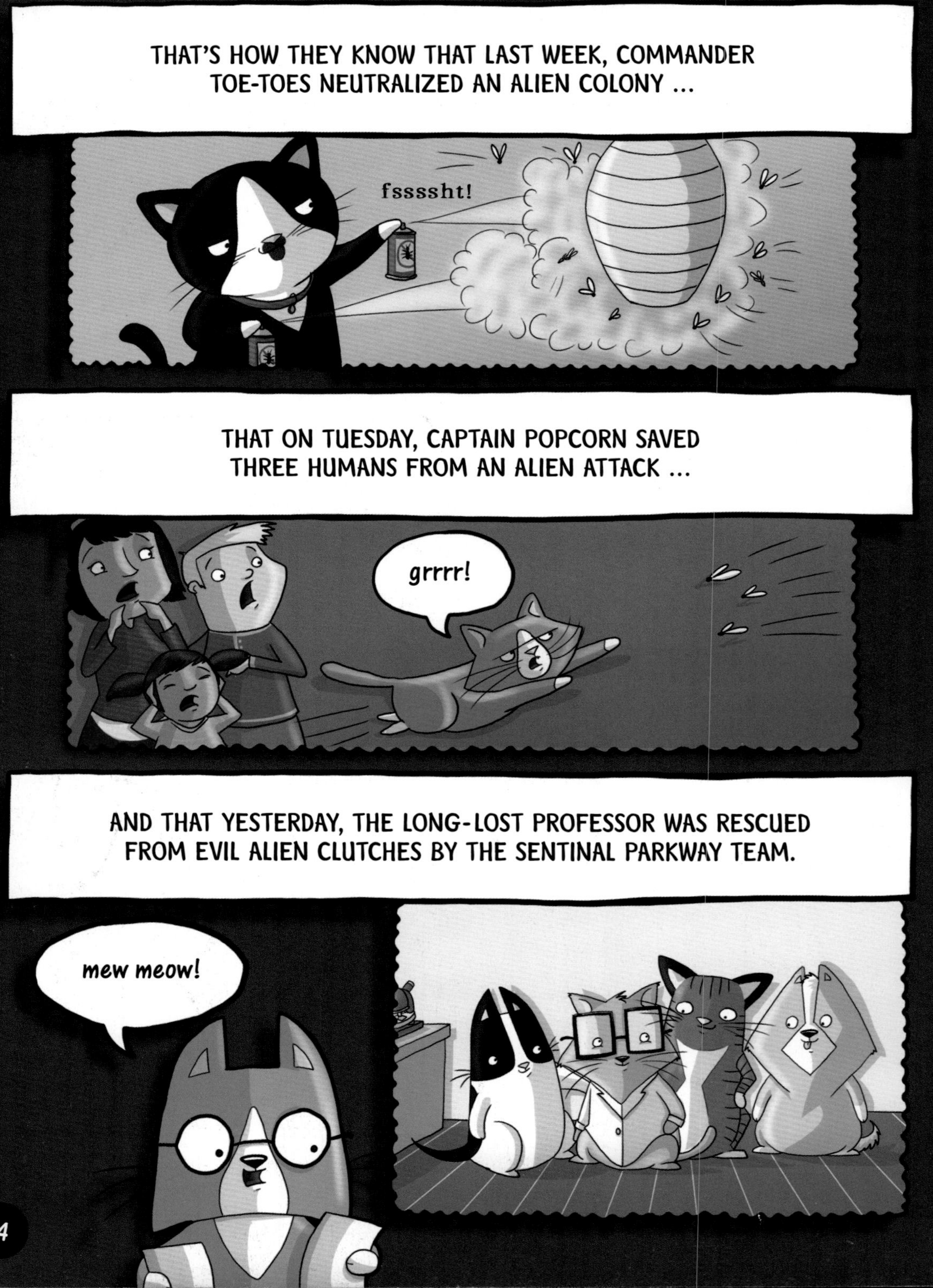
THAT'S HOW THEY KNOW THAT LAST WEEK, COMMANDER TOE-TOES NEUTRALIZED AN ALIEN COLONY ...
fssssht!
THAT ON TUESDAY, CAPTAIN POPCORN SAVED THREE HUMANS FROM AN ALIEN ATTACK ...
grrrr!
AND THAT YESTERDAY, THE LONG-LOST PROFESSOR WAS RESCUED FROM EVIL ALIEN CLUTCHES BY THE SENTINAL PARKWAY TEAM.
mew meow!

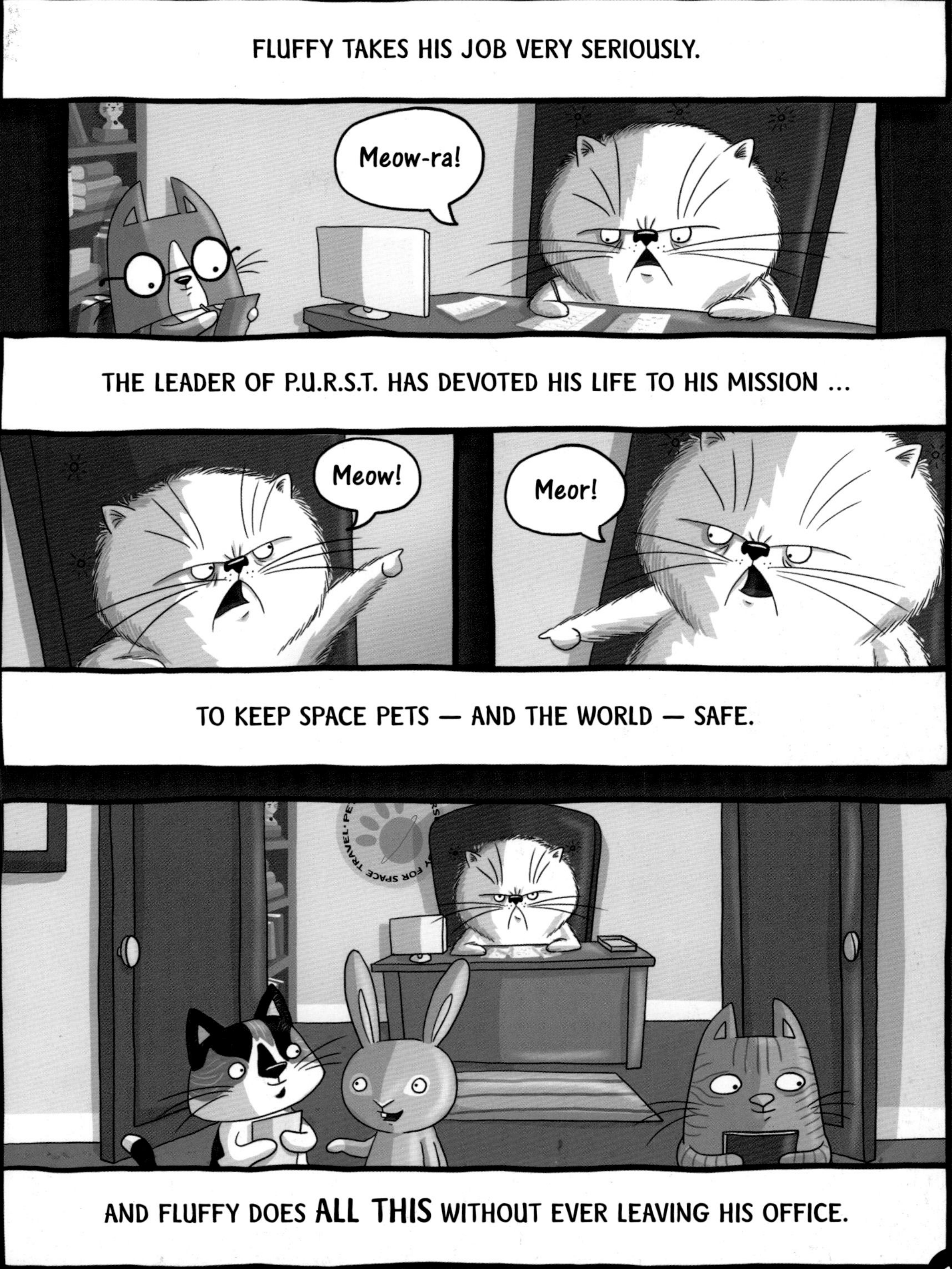
FLUFFY TAKES HIS JOB VERY SERIOUSLY.
Meow-ra!
THE LEADER OF P.U.R.S.T. HAS DEVOTED HIS LIFE TO HIS MISSION ...
Meow!
Meor!
TO KEEP SPACE PETS — AND THE WORLD — SAFE.
AND FLUFFY DOES ALL THIS WITHOUT EVER LEAVING HIS OFFICE.

HE WASN'T ALWAYS BEHIND A DESK.

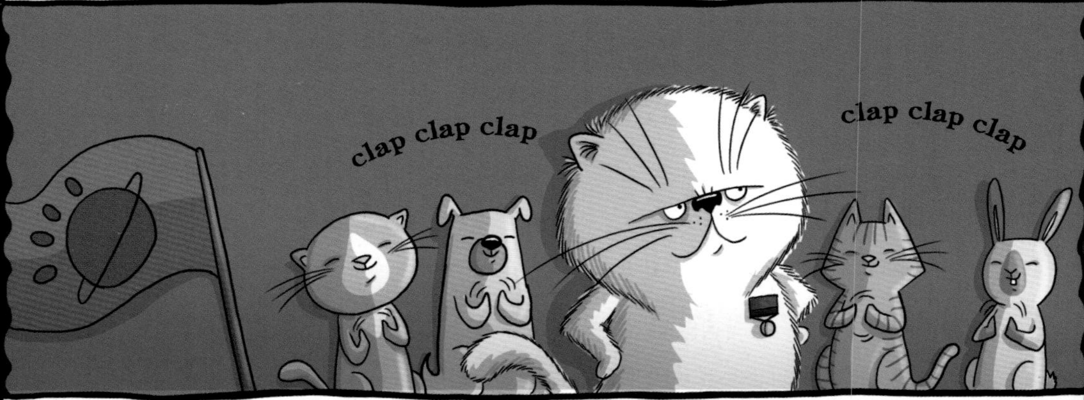
clap clap clap
clap clap clap

HE WAS ONCE A SKILLED OPERATIVE OF P.U.R.S.T. HIMSELF.

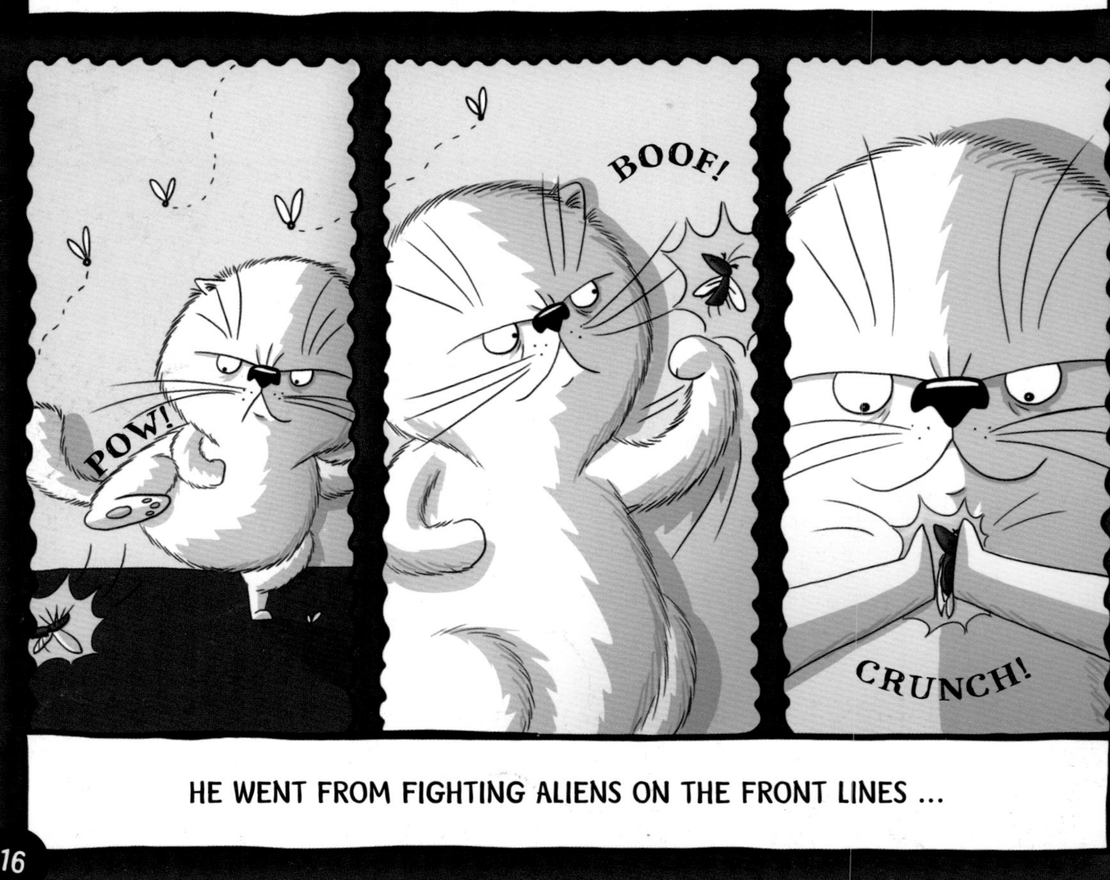
POW!
BOOF!
CRUNCH!

HE WENT FROM FIGHTING ALIENS ON THE FRONT LINES ...

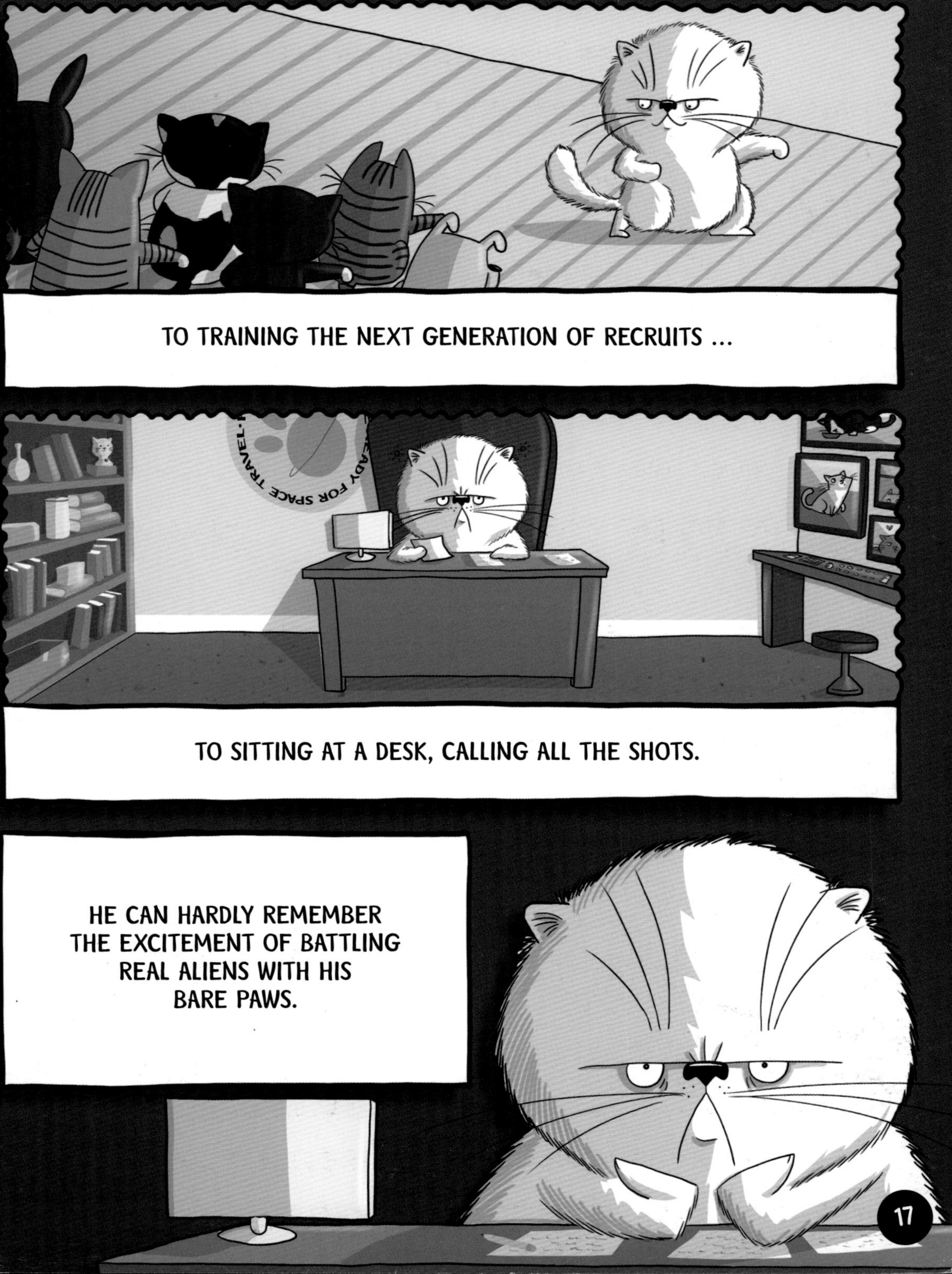
TO TRAINING THE NEXT GENERATION OF RECRUITS ...
TO SITTING AT A DESK, CALLING ALL THE SHOTS.
HE CAN HARDLY REMEMBER THE EXCITEMENT OF BATTLING REAL ALIENS WITH HIS BARE PAWS.

FLUFFY HAS DONE HIS BEST TO STAY IN SHAPE.

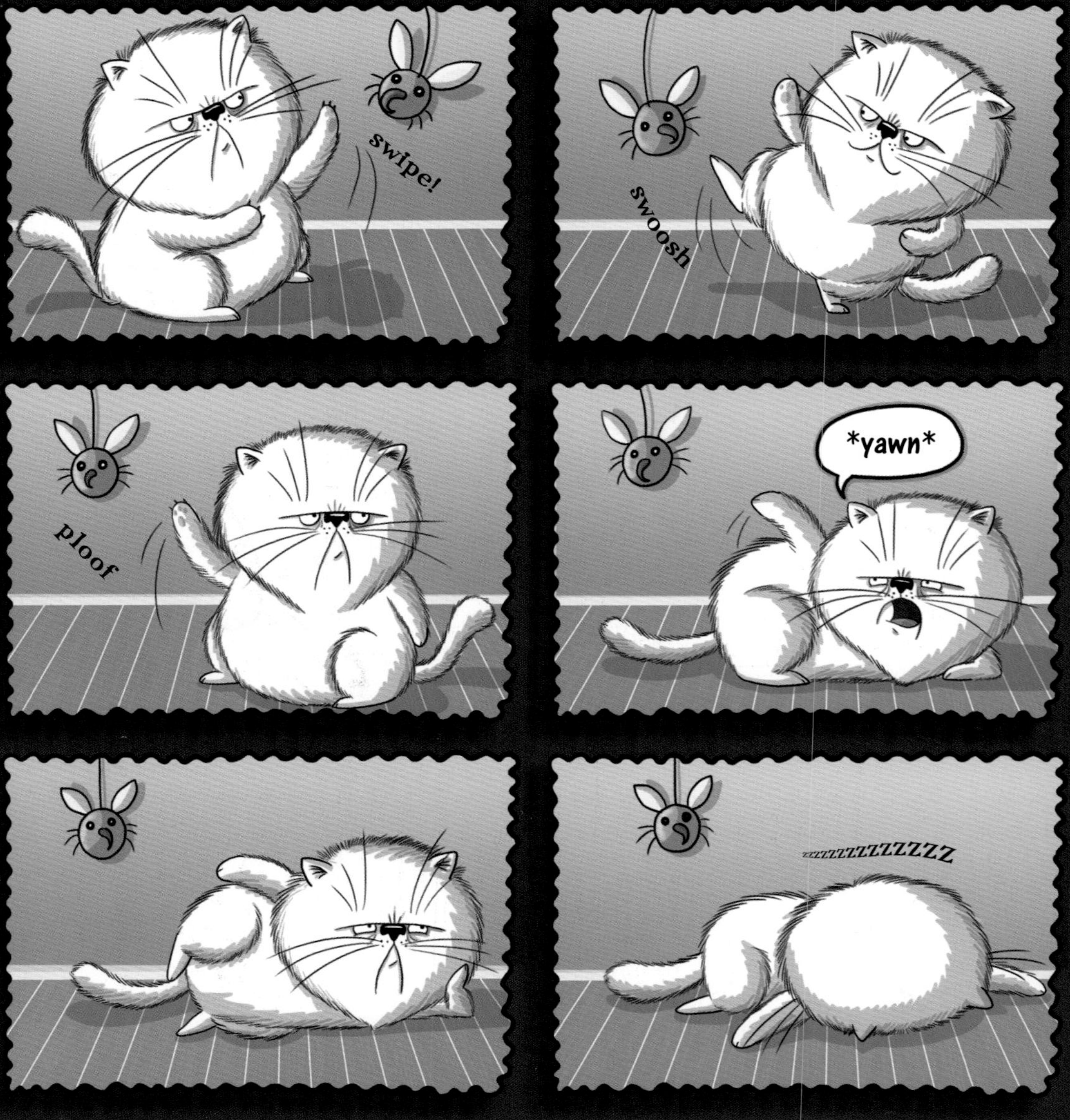
swipe!
swoosh
ploof
yawn

BUT LIVING IN THE SAFEST, MOST SECURE BUILDING IN THE WORLD CAN MAKE A CAT KIND OF LAZY.

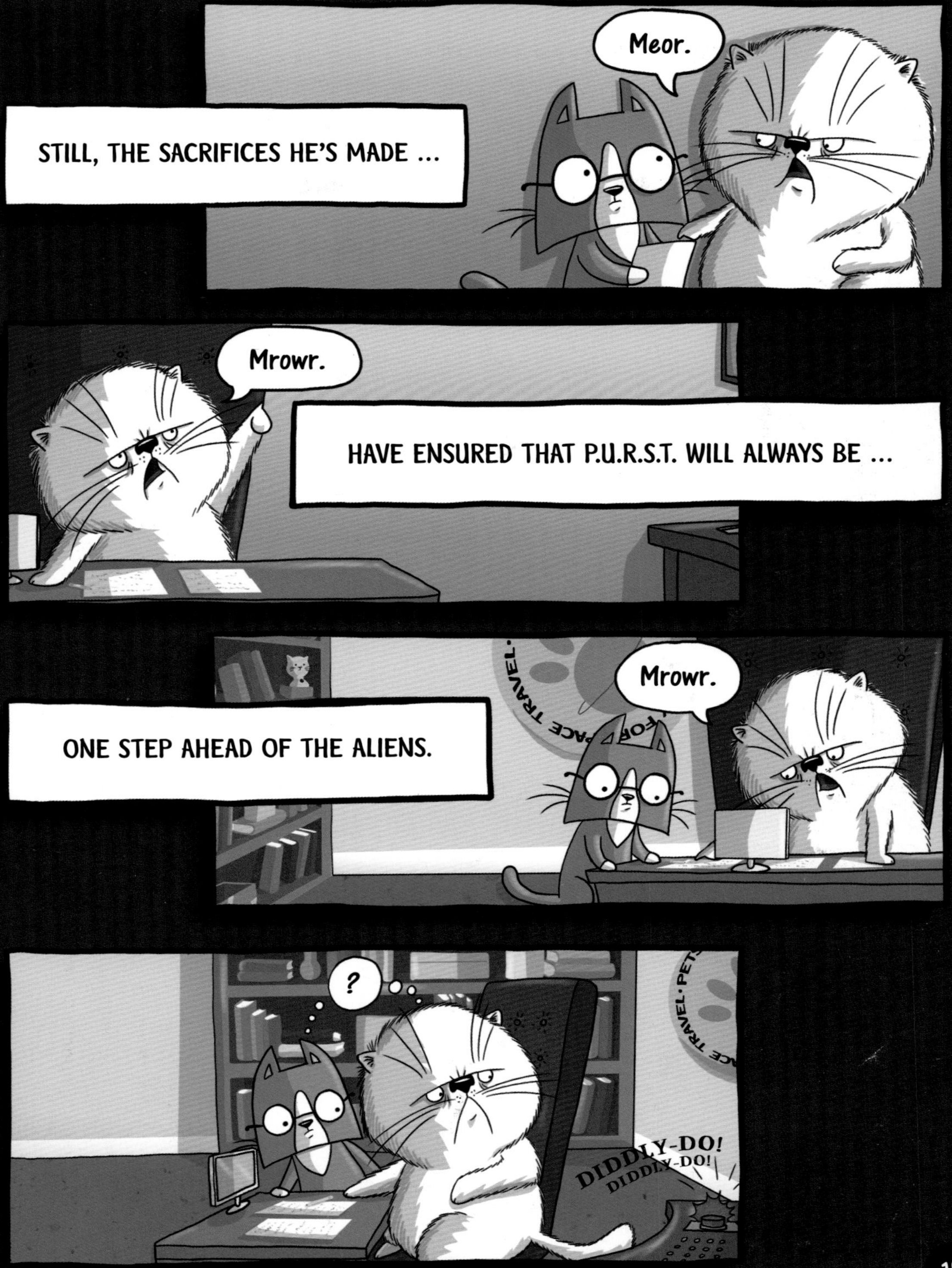
STILL, THE SACRIFICES HE'S MADE ...
Meor.
Mrowr.
HAVE ENSURED THAT P.U.R.S.T. WILL ALWAYS BE ...
ONE STEP AHEAD OF THE ALIENS.
Mrowr.
?
DIDDLY-DO!
DIDDLY-DO!

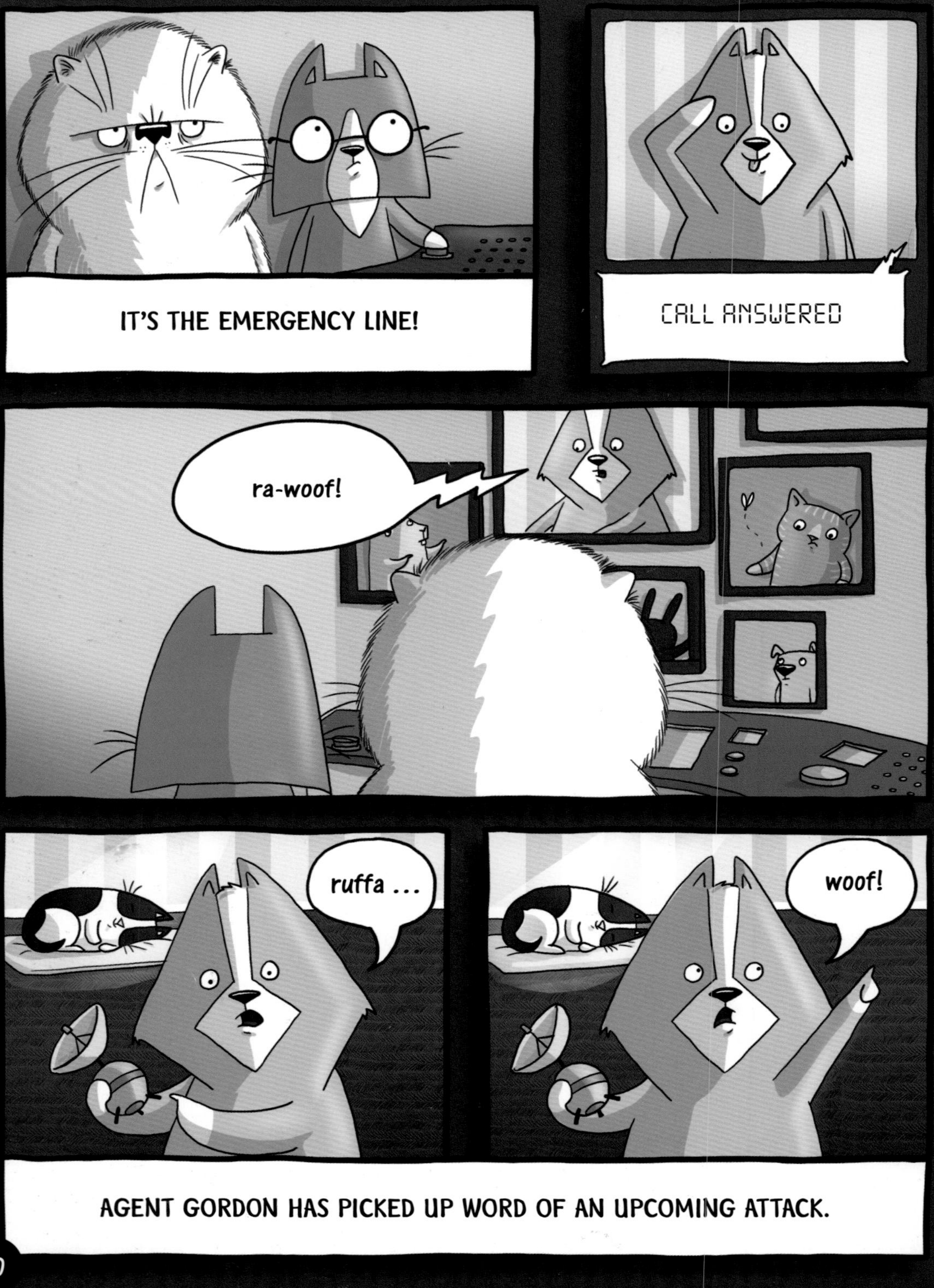
IT'S THE EMERGENCY LINE!
CALL ANSWERED
ra-woof!
ruffa ...
woof!
AGENT GORDON HAS PICKED UP WORD OF AN UPCOMING ATTACK.

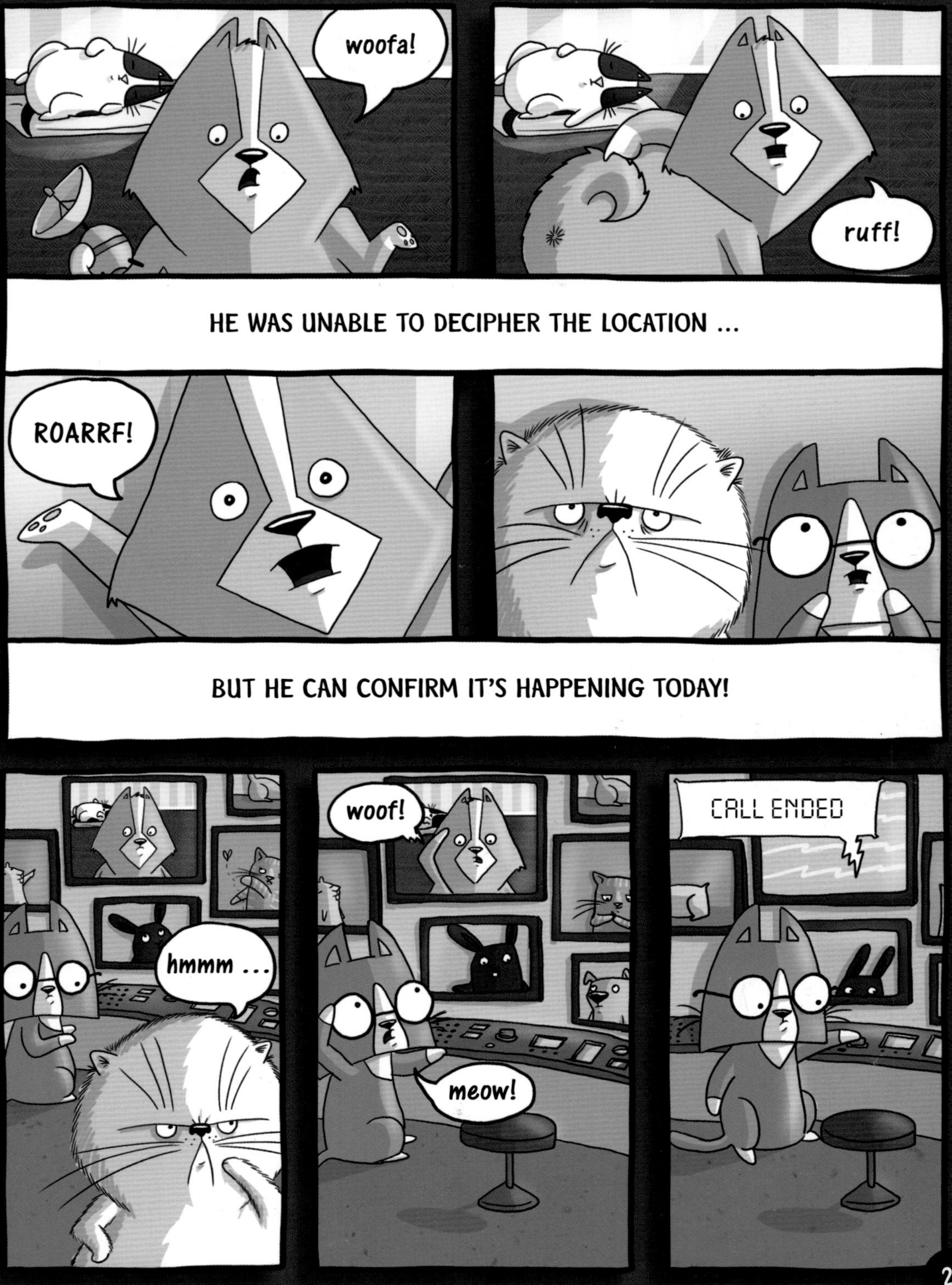
woofa!
ruff!
HE WAS UNABLE TO DECIPHER THE LOCATION ...
ROARRF!
BUT HE CAN CONFIRM IT'S HAPPENING TODAY!
hmmm ...
woof!
meow!
CALL ENDED

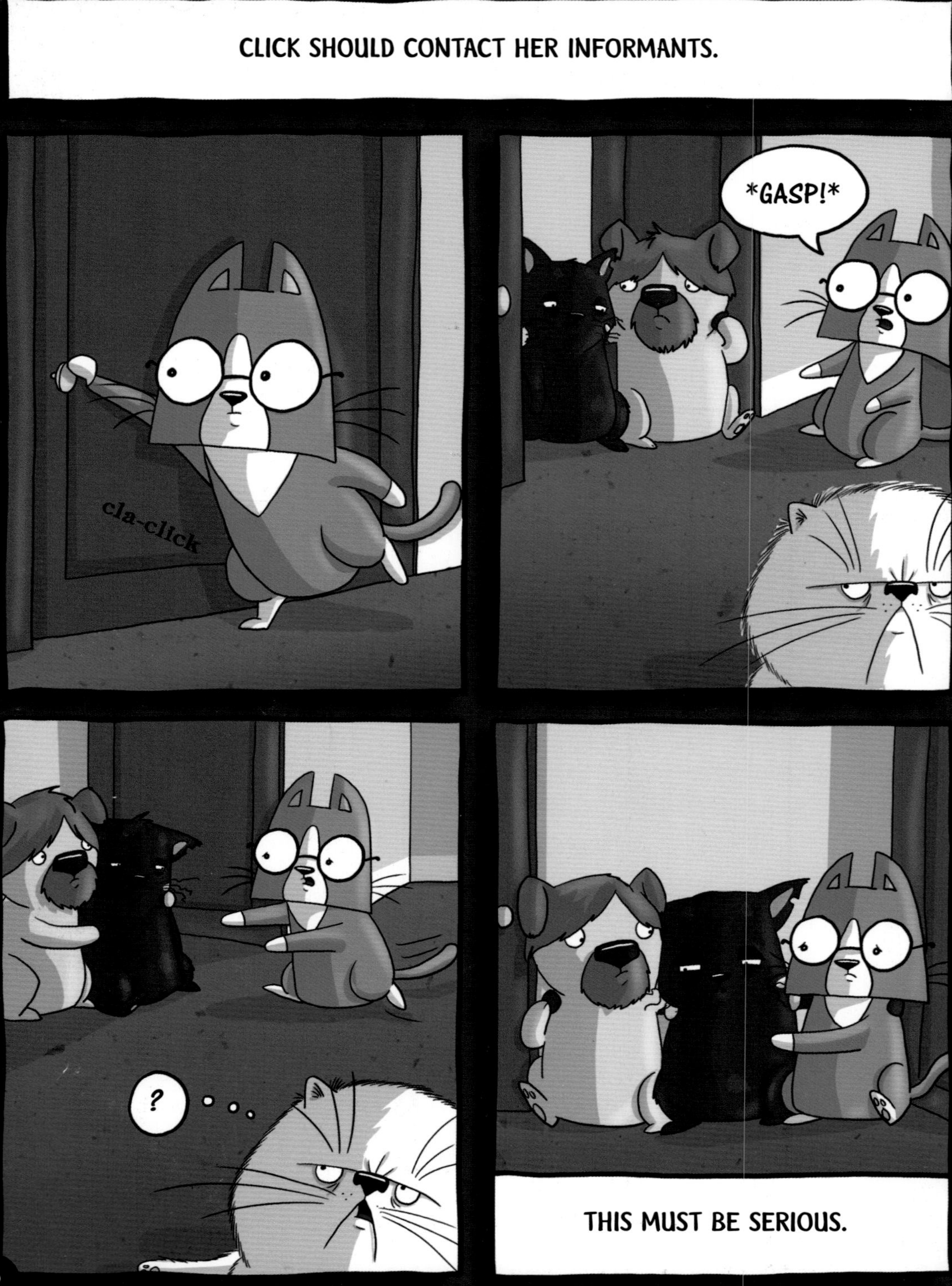
CLICK SHOULD CONTACT HER INFORMANTS.
cla-click
GASP!
?
THIS MUST BE SERIOUS.

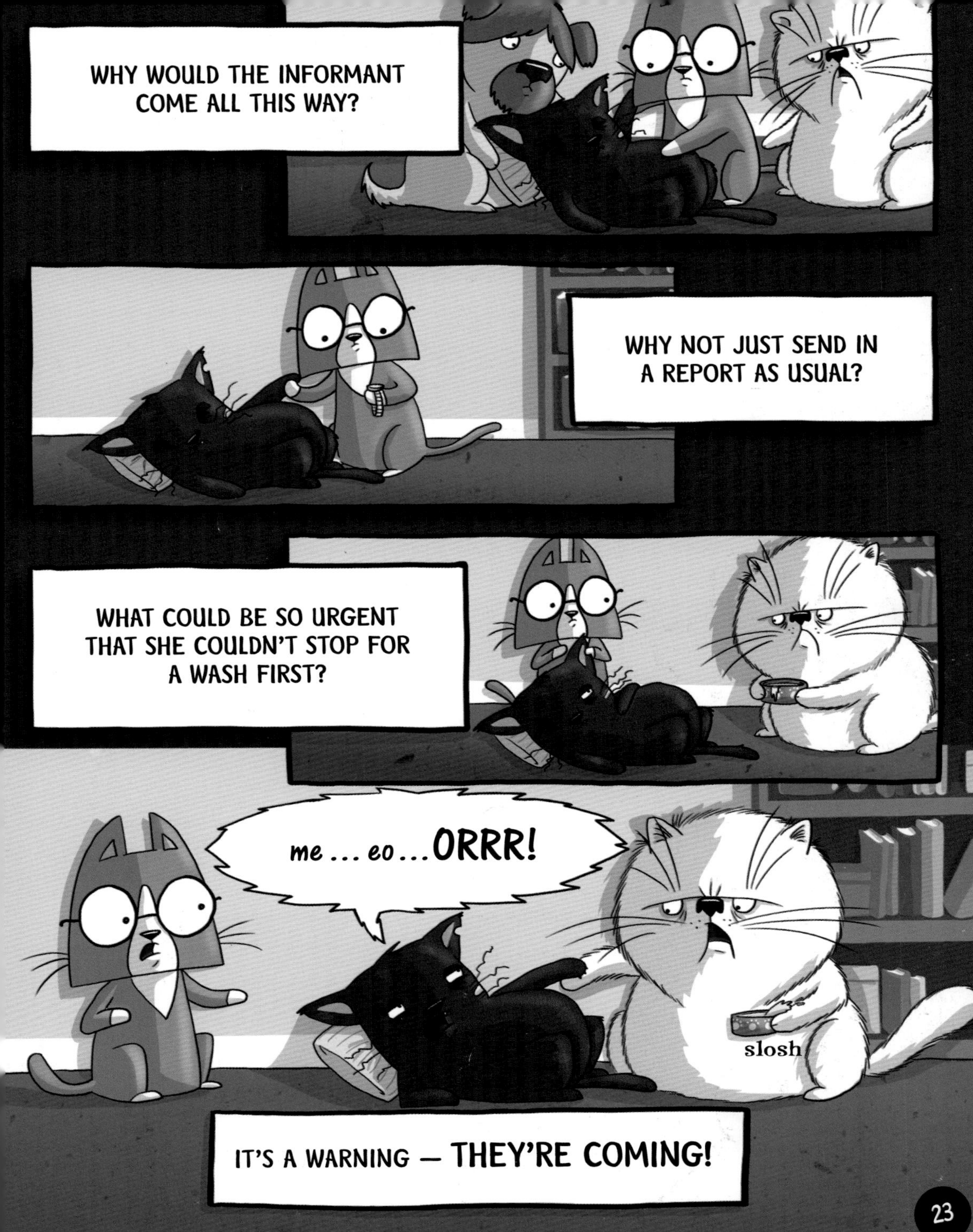
WHY WOULD THE INFORMANT COME ALL THIS WAY?
WHY NOT JUST SEND IN A REPORT AS USUAL?
WHAT COULD BE SO URGENT THAT SHE COULDN'T STOP FOR A WASH FIRST?
me ... eo ... ORRR!
slosh
IT'S A WARNING — THEY'RE COMING!

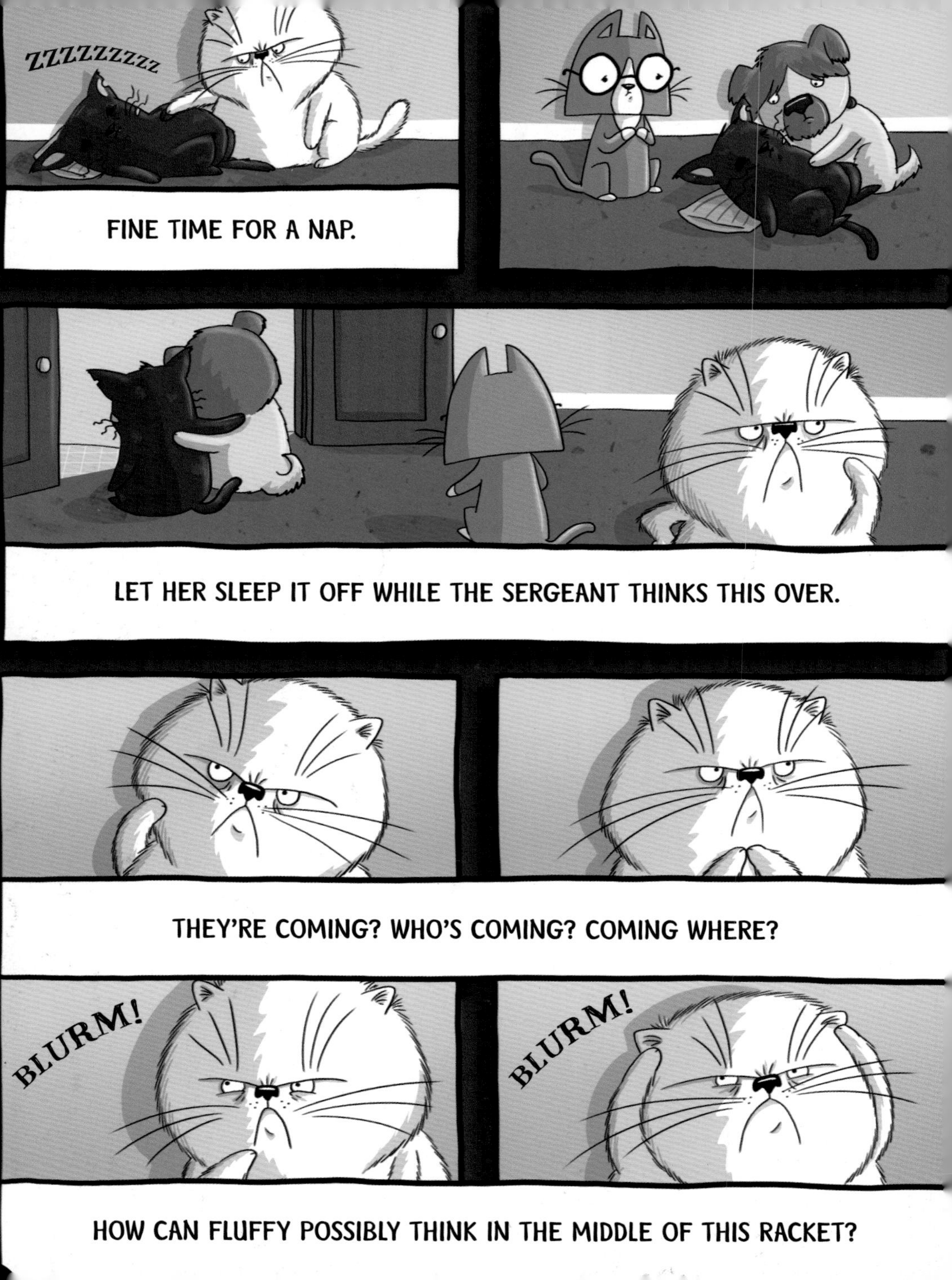
ZZZZZZZZZ
FINE TIME FOR A NAP.
LET HER SLEEP IT OFF WHILE THE SERGEANT THINKS THIS OVER.
THEY'RE COMING? WHO'S COMING? COMING WHERE?
BLURM!
BLURM!
HOW CAN FLUFFY POSSIBLY THINK IN THE MIDDLE OF THIS RACKET?

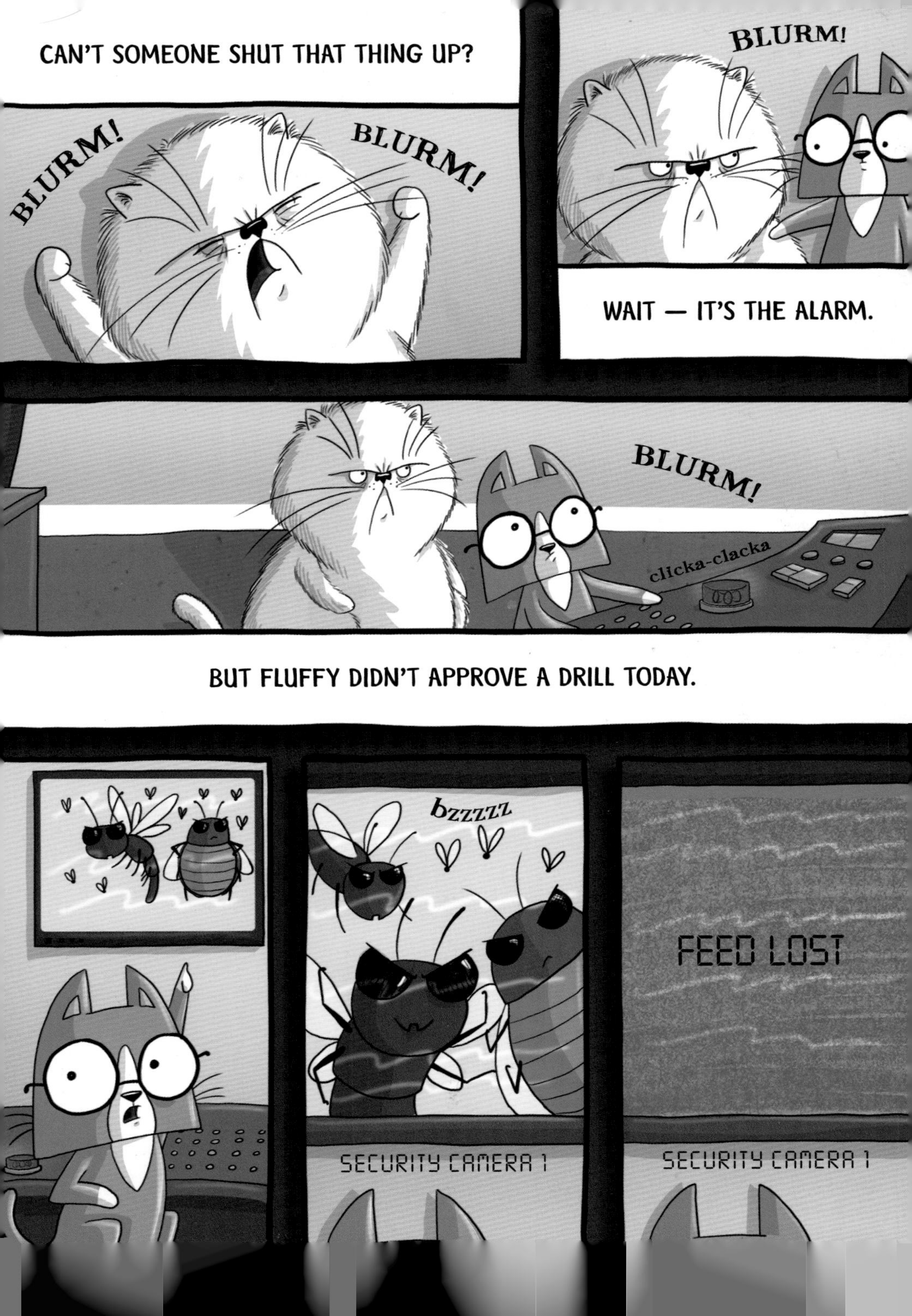

CAN'T SOMEONE SHUT THAT THING UP?
BLURM!
BLURM!
BLURM!
WAIT — IT'S THE ALARM.
BLURM!
clicka-clacka
BUT FLUFFY DIDN'T APPROVE A DRILL TODAY.
bzzzzz
SECURITY CAMERA 1
FEED LOST
SECURITY CAMERA 1

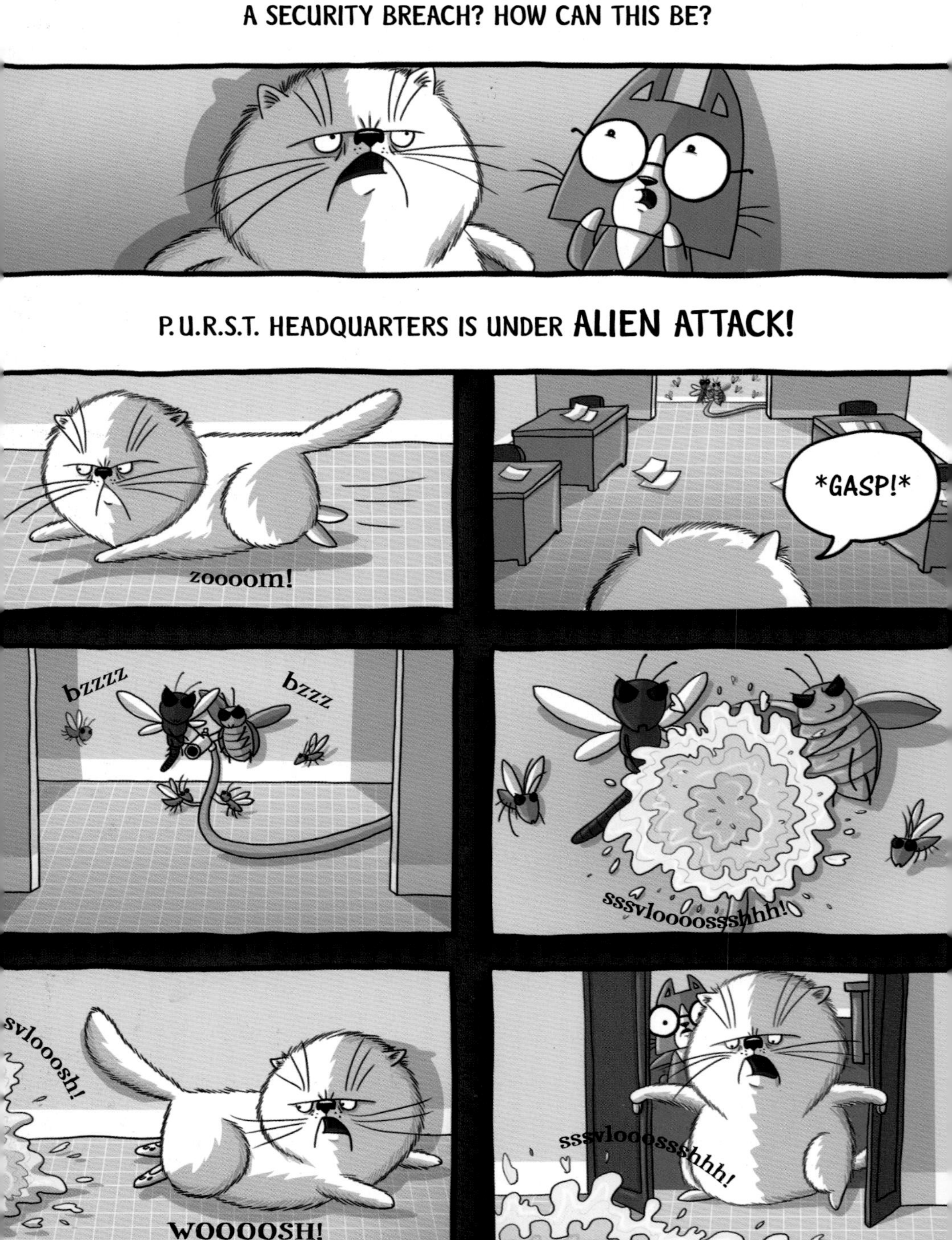
A SECURITY BREACH? HOW CAN THIS BE?
P.U.R.S.T. HEADQUARTERS IS UNDER ALIEN ATTACK!
zoooom!
GASP!
bzzzz
bzzz
sssvloooosssshhh!
svlooosh!
WOOOOSH!
sssvlooossshhh!

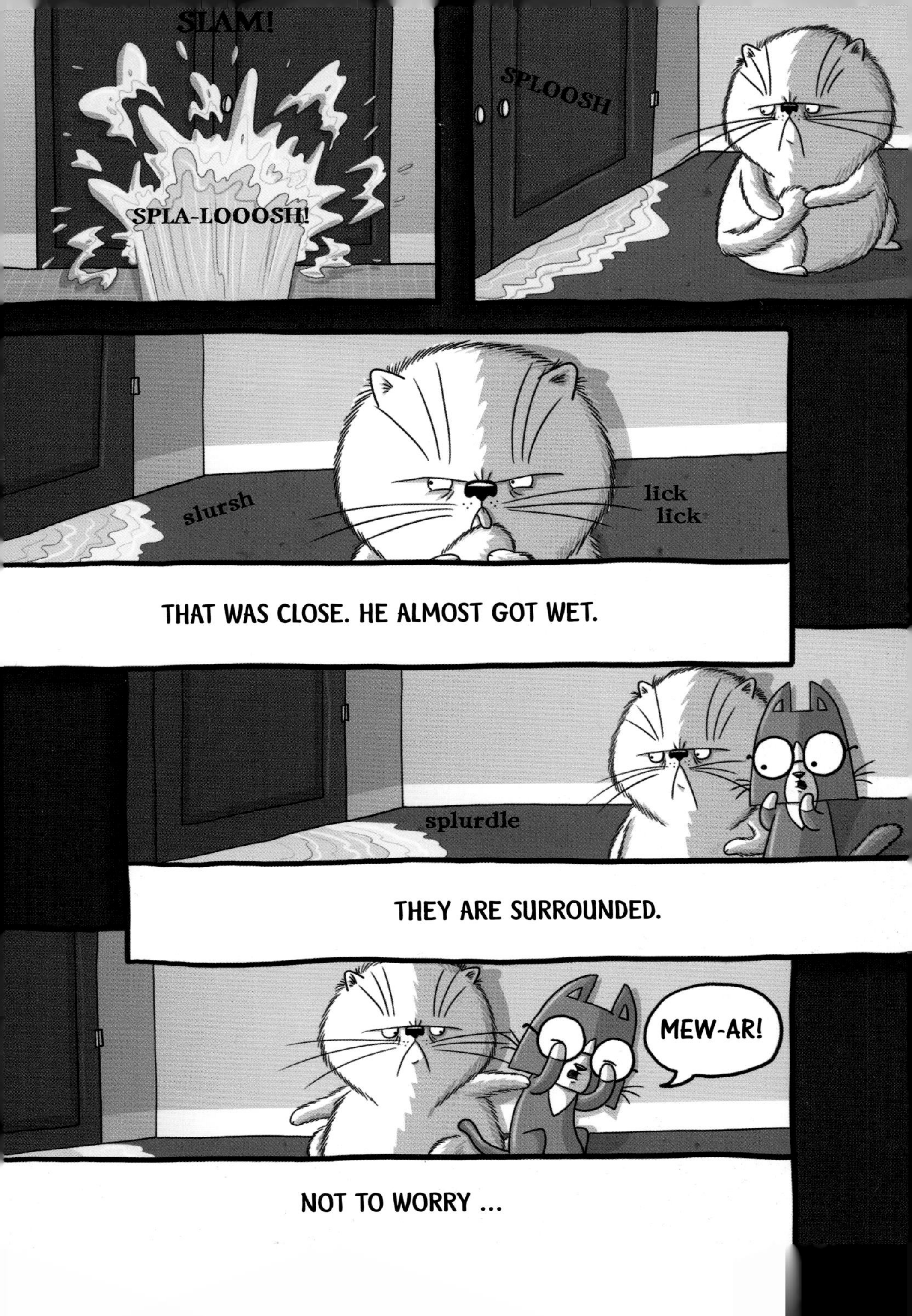
SLAM!
SPLA-LOOOSH!
SPLOOSH
slursh
lick
lick
THAT WAS CLOSE. HE ALMOST GOT WET.
splurdle
THEY ARE SURROUNDED.
MEW-AR!
NOT TO WORRY ...

SERGEANT FLUFFY VANDERMERE ISN'T GOING DOWN THAT EASILY.

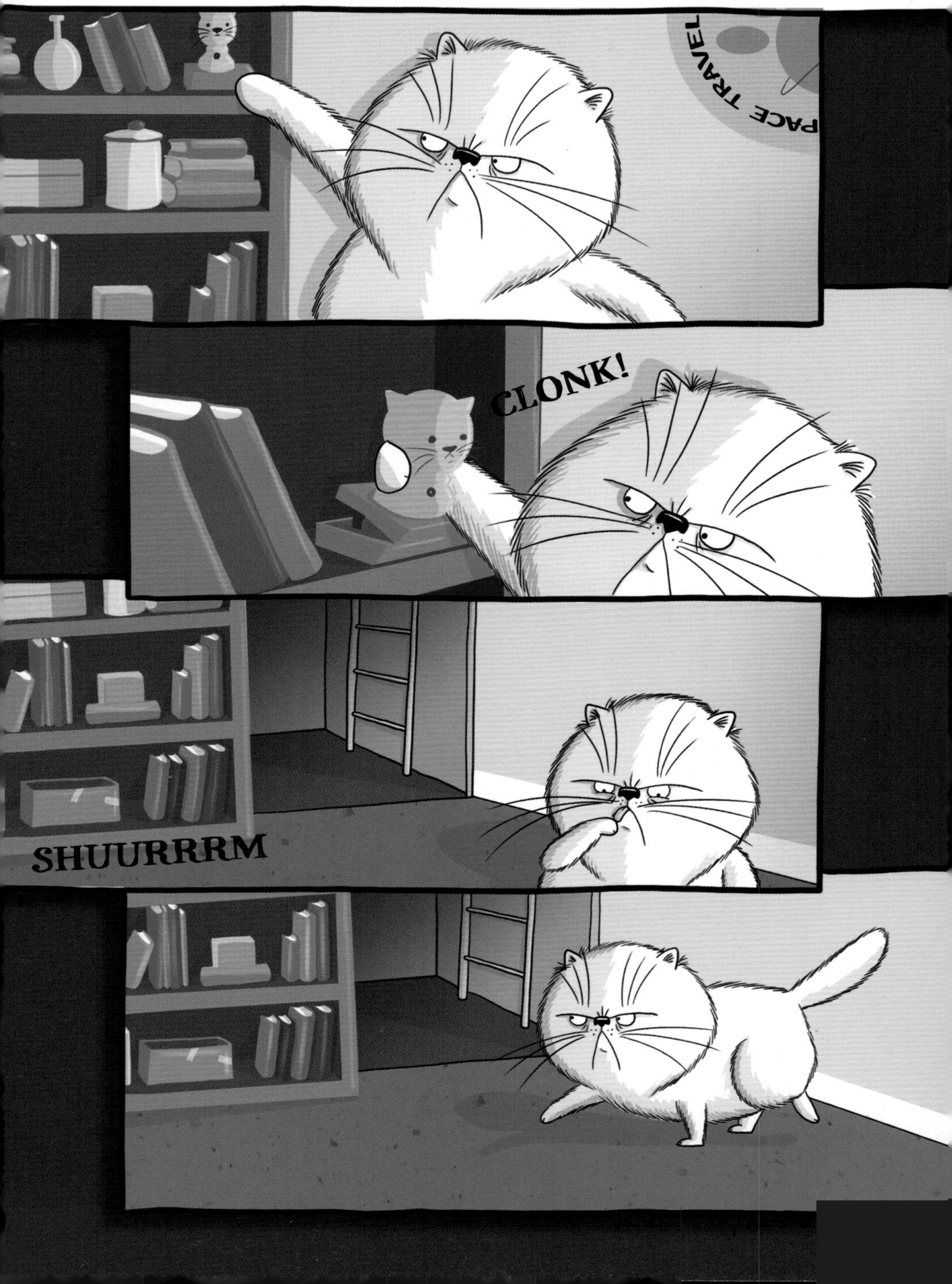
PACE TRAVEL
CLONK!
SHUURRRM

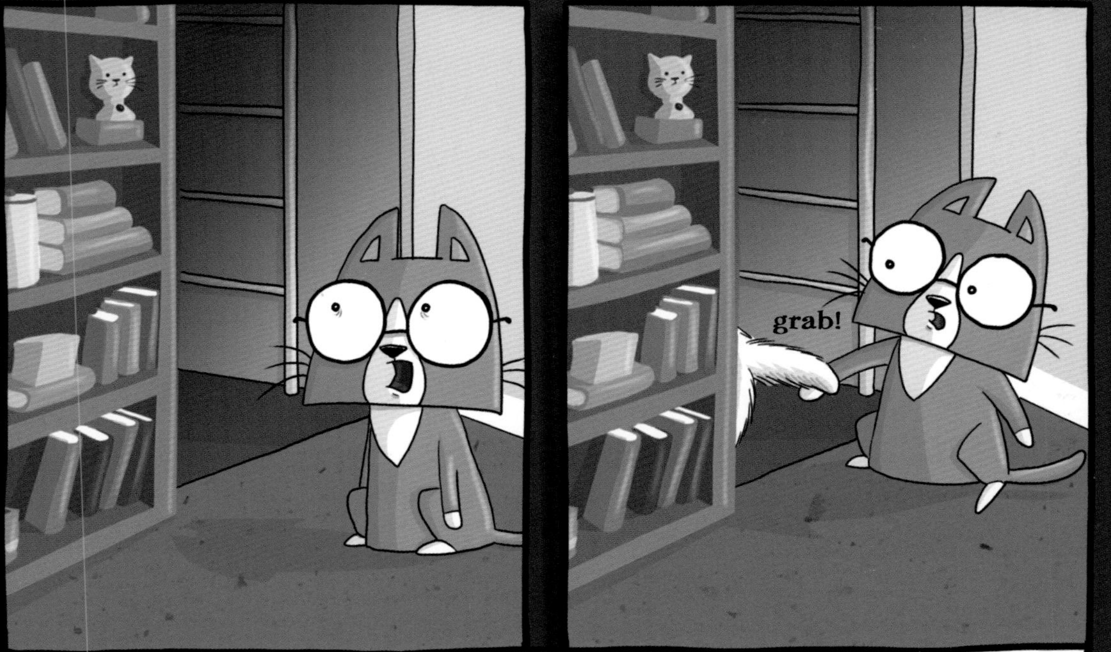
grab!

AND HE'S NOT GOING TO LET THEM GET HIS SECOND IN COMMAND EITHER.

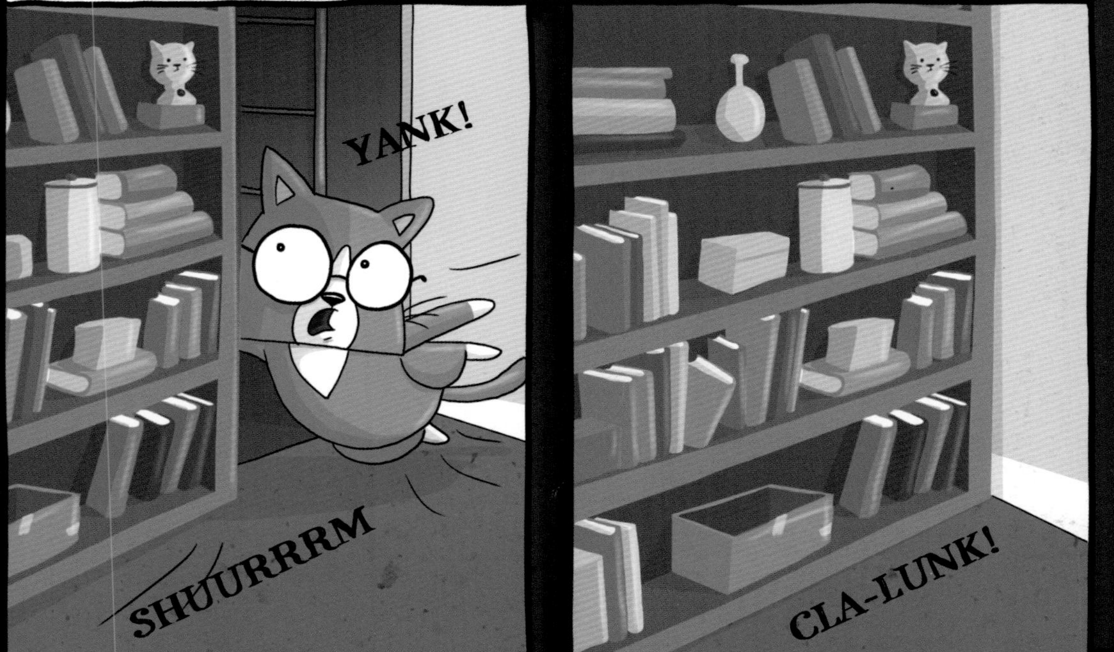
YANK!
SHUURRRM
CLA-LUNK!

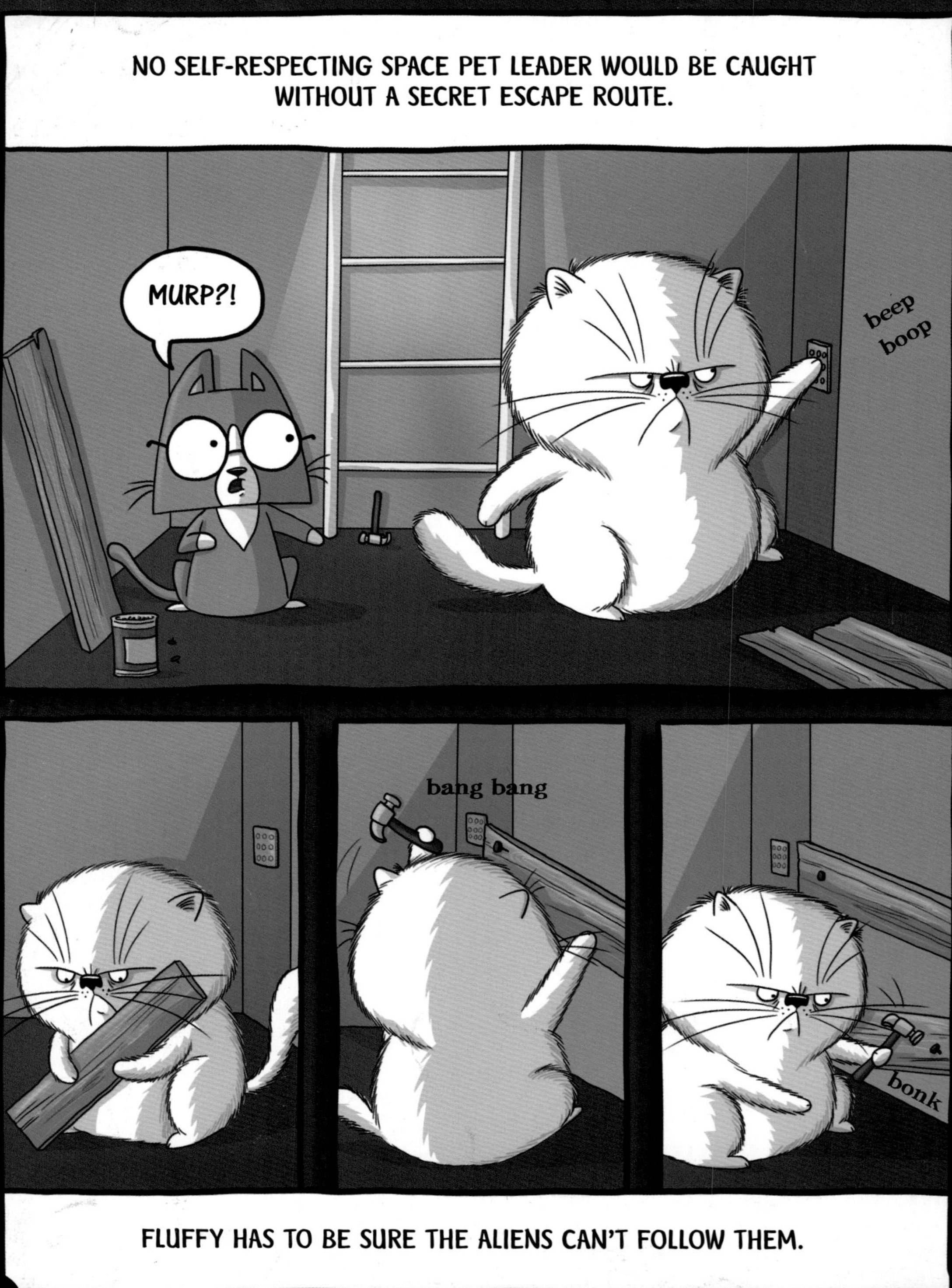
NO SELF-RESPECTING SPACE PET LEADER WOULD BE CAUGHT WITHOUT A SECRET ESCAPE ROUTE.
MURP?!
beep boop
bang bang
bonk
FLUFFY HAS TO BE SURE THE ALIENS CAN'T FOLLOW THEM.

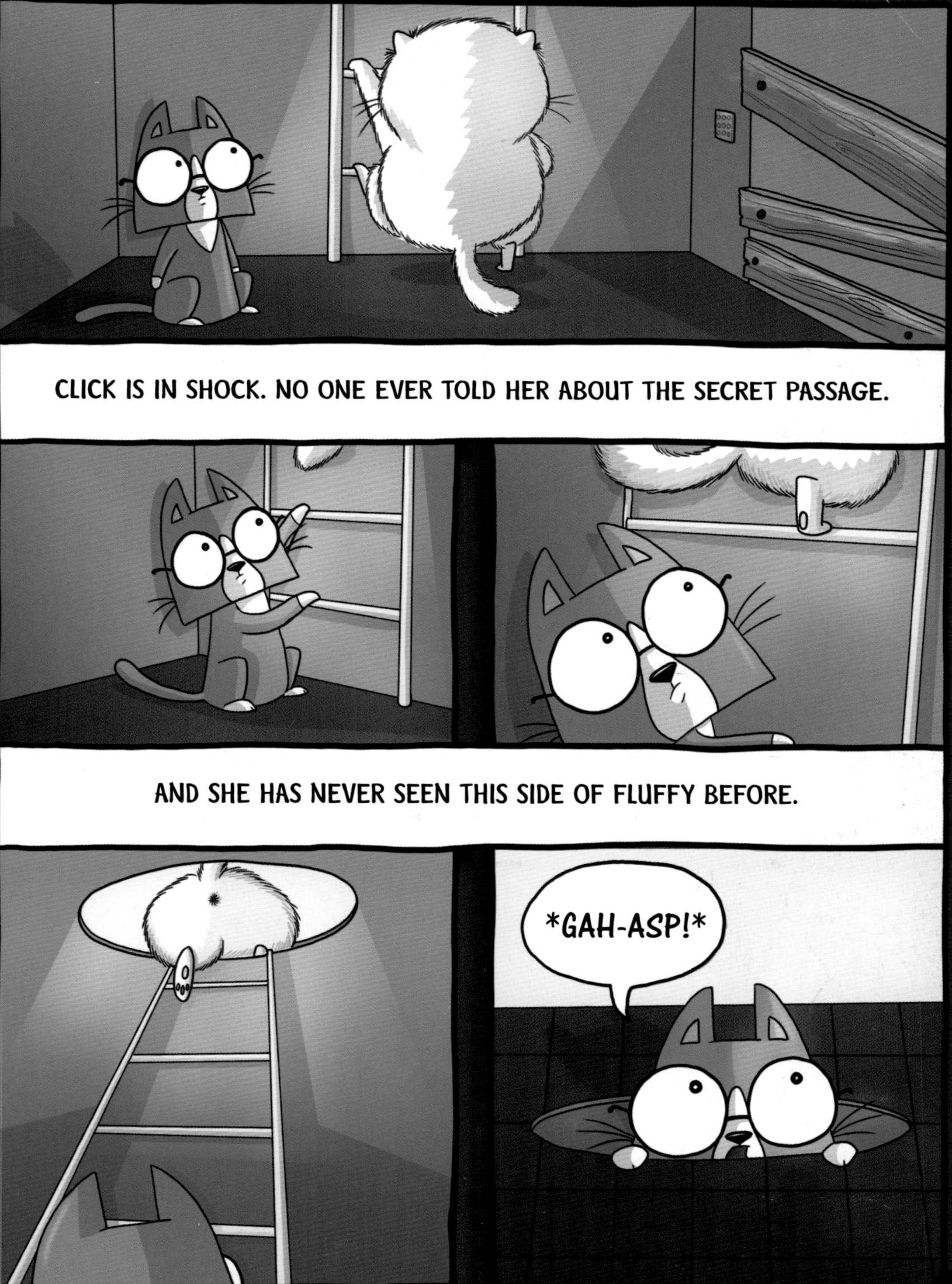
CLICK IS IN SHOCK. NO ONE EVER TOLD HER ABOUT THE SECRET PASSAGE.
AND SHE HAS NEVER SEEN THIS SIDE OF FLUFFY BEFORE.
GAH-ASP!

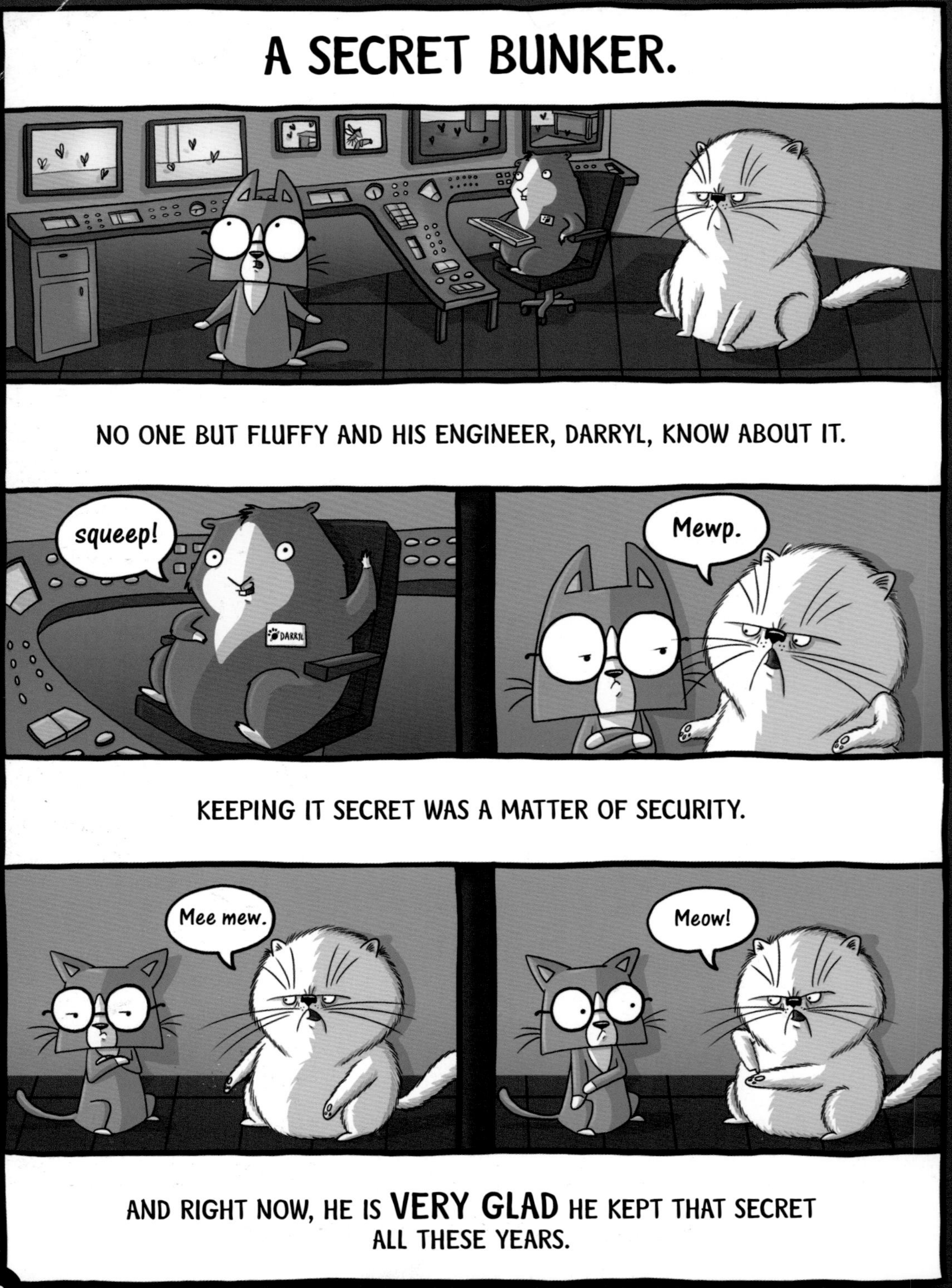
A SECRET BUNKER.
NO ONE BUT FLUFFY AND HIS ENGINEER, DARRYL, KNOW ABOUT IT.
squeep!
DARRYL
Mewp.
KEEPING IT SECRET WAS A MATTER OF SECURITY.
Mee mew.
Meow!
AND RIGHT NOW, HE IS VERY GLAD HE KEPT THAT SECRET
ALL THESE YEARS.

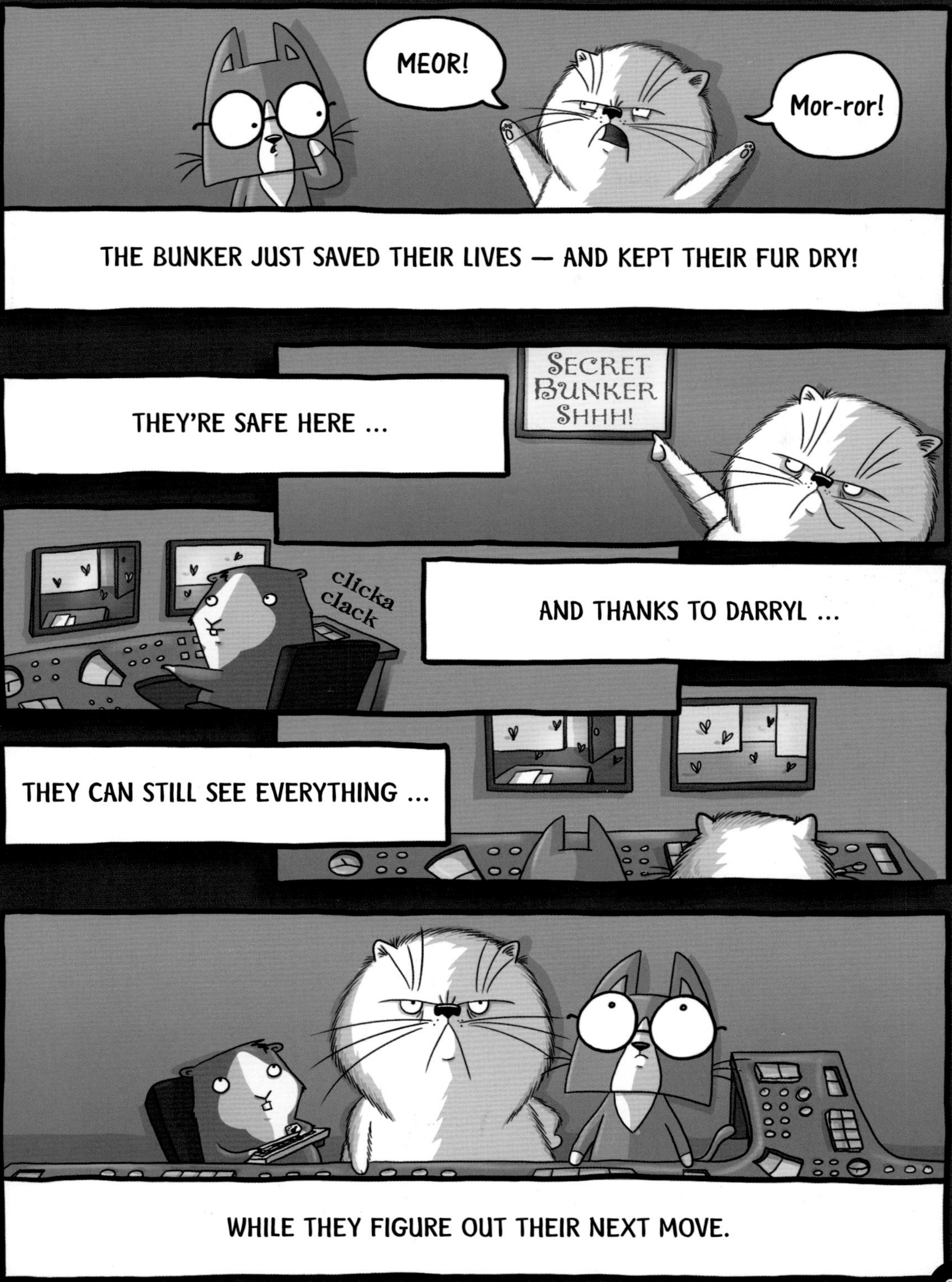
MEOR!
Mor-ror!
THE BUNKER JUST SAVED THEIR LIVES — AND KEPT THEIR FUR DRY!
THEY'RE SAFE HERE ...
SECRET BUNKER SHHH!
clicka clack
AND THANKS TO DARRYL ...
THEY CAN STILL SEE EVERYTHING ...
WHILE THEY FIGURE OUT THEIR NEXT MOVE.

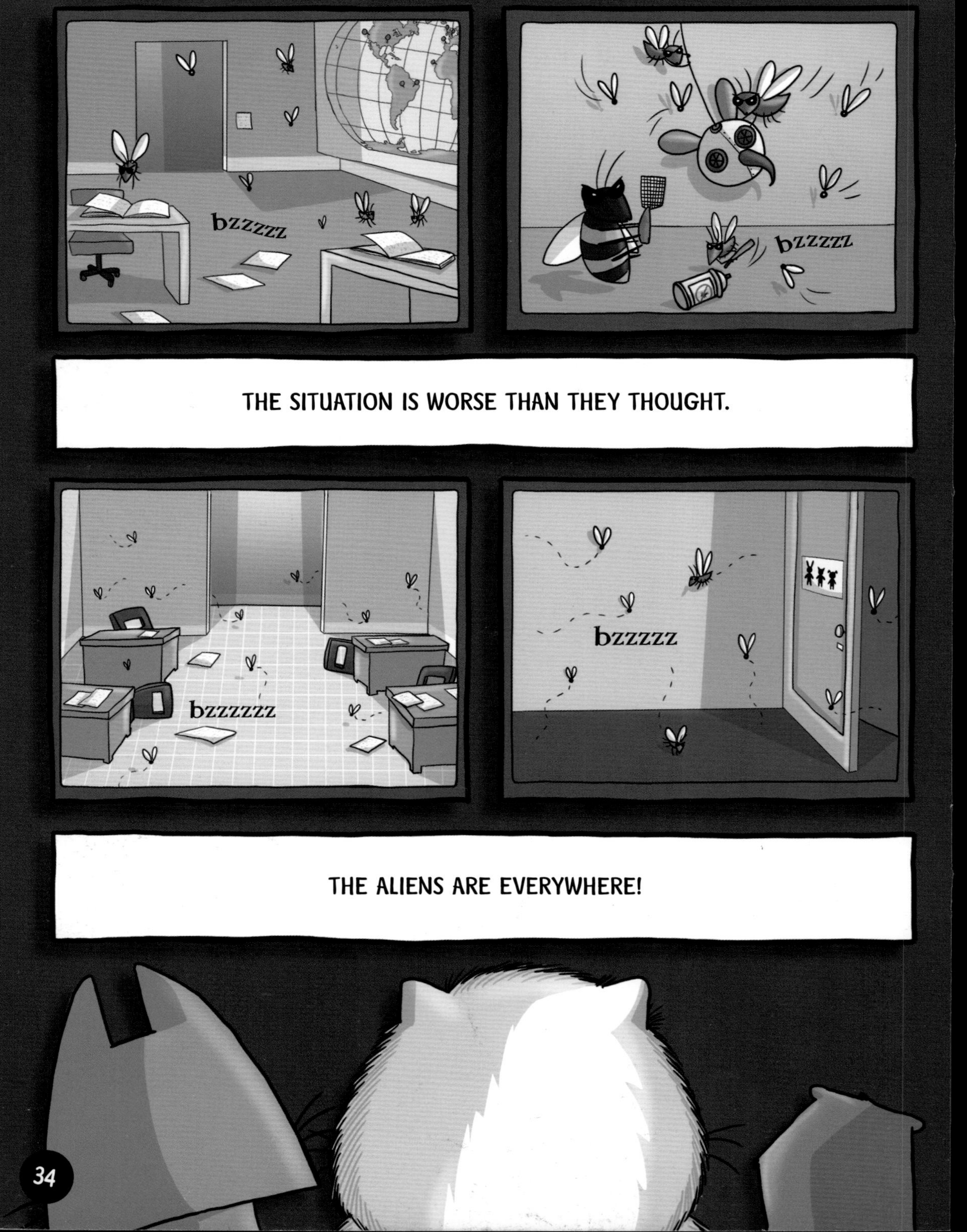
bzzzzz
bzzzzz
THE SITUATION IS WORSE THAN THEY THOUGHT.
bzzzzzz
bzzzzz
THE ALIENS ARE EVERYWHERE!

THEY'VE TAKEN HOSTAGES!

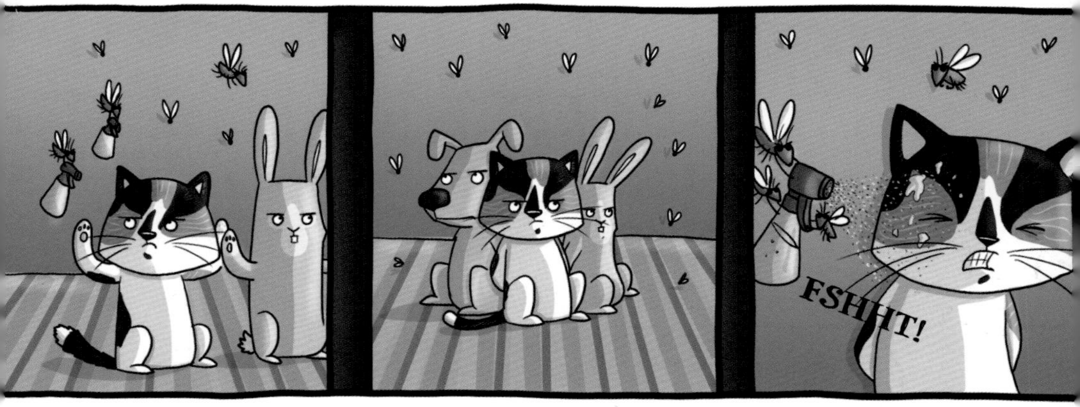
FSHHT!

AND THEY'RE TORTURING THEM!

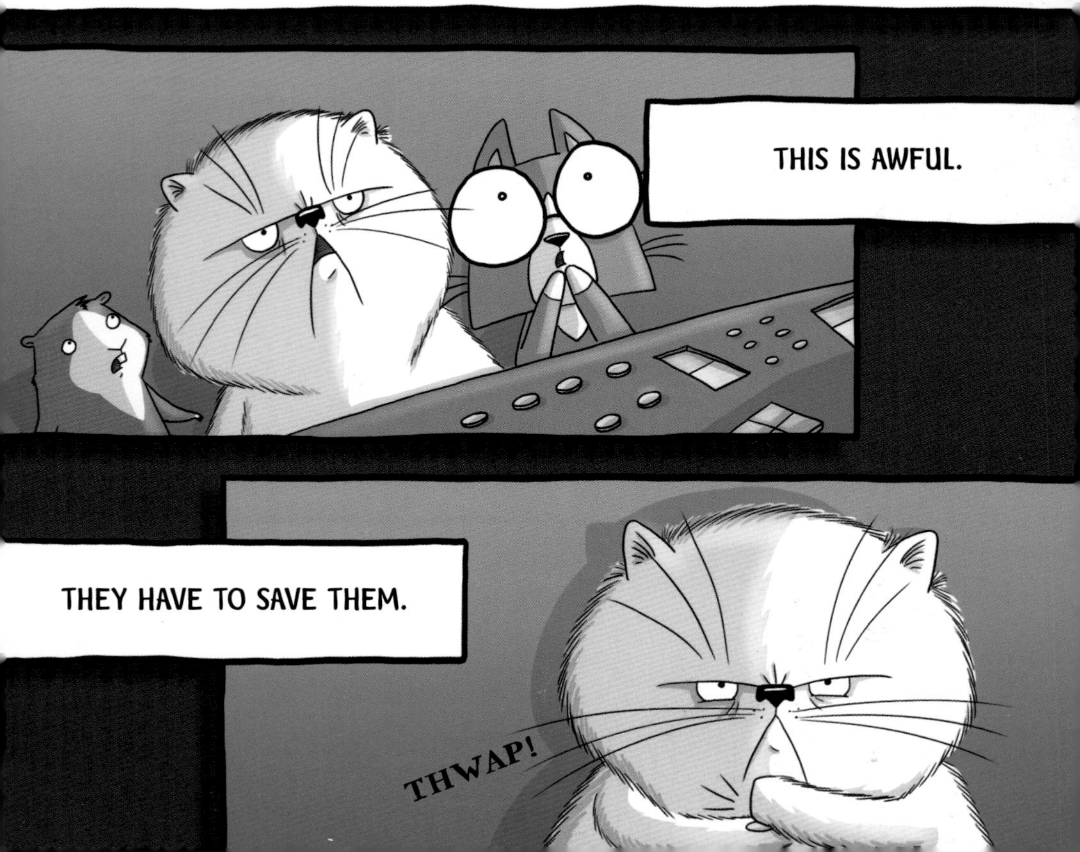
THIS IS AWFUL.
THEY HAVE TO SAVE THEM.
THWAP!

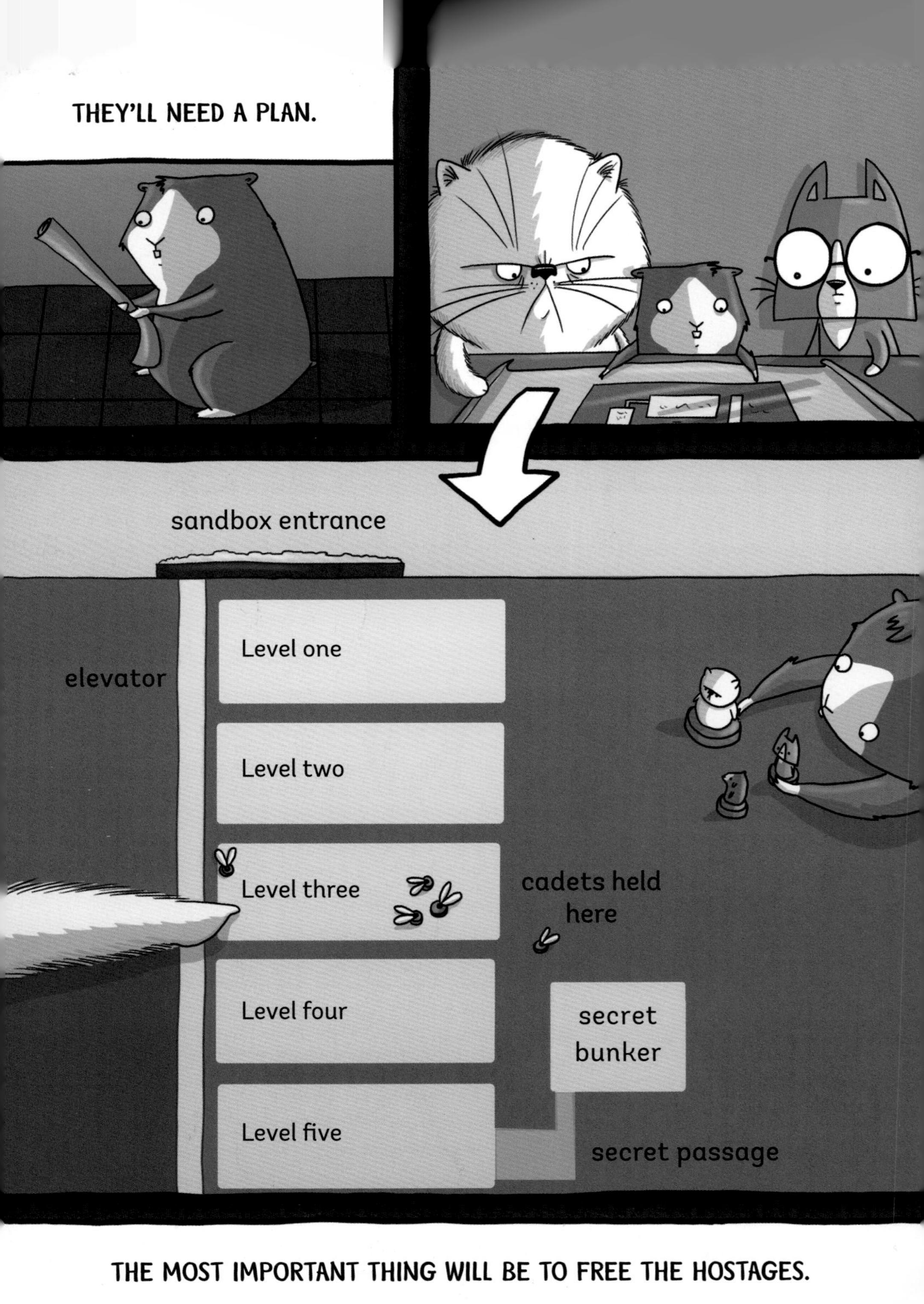
THEY'LL NEED A PLAN.
sandbox entrance
elevator
Level one
Level two
Level three
Level four
Level five
cadets held here
secret bunker
secret passage
THE MOST IMPORTANT THING WILL BE TO FREE THE HOSTAGES.

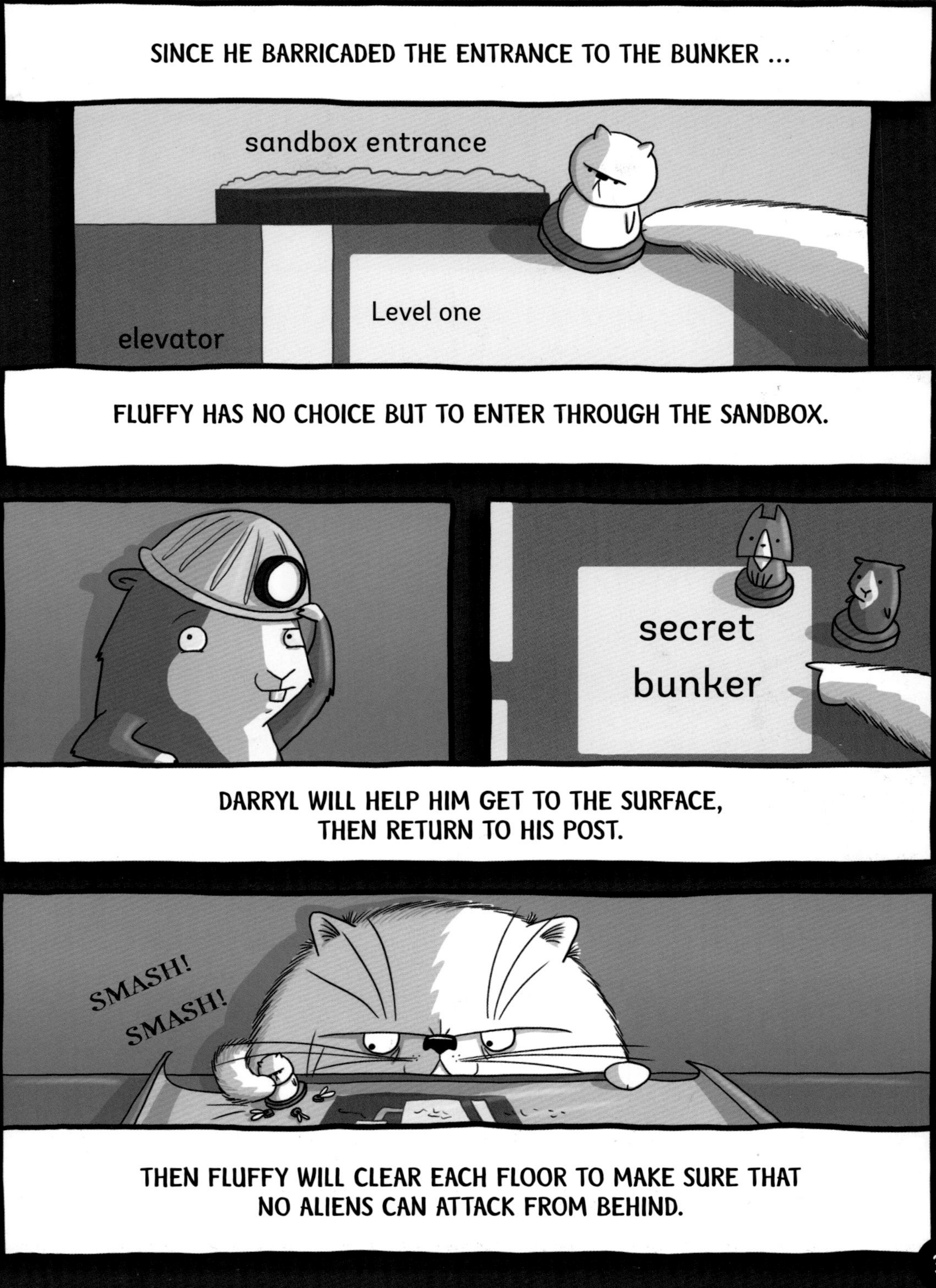
SINCE HE BARRICADED THE ENTRANCE TO THE BUNKER ...
sandbox entrance
elevator
Level one
FLUFFY HAS NO CHOICE BUT TO ENTER THROUGH THE SANDBOX.
secret bunker
DARRYL WILL HELP HIM GET TO THE SURFACE, THEN RETURN TO HIS POST.
SMASH!
SMASH!
THEN FLUFFY WILL CLEAR EACH FLOOR TO MAKE SURE THAT NO ALIENS CAN ATTACK FROM BEHIND.

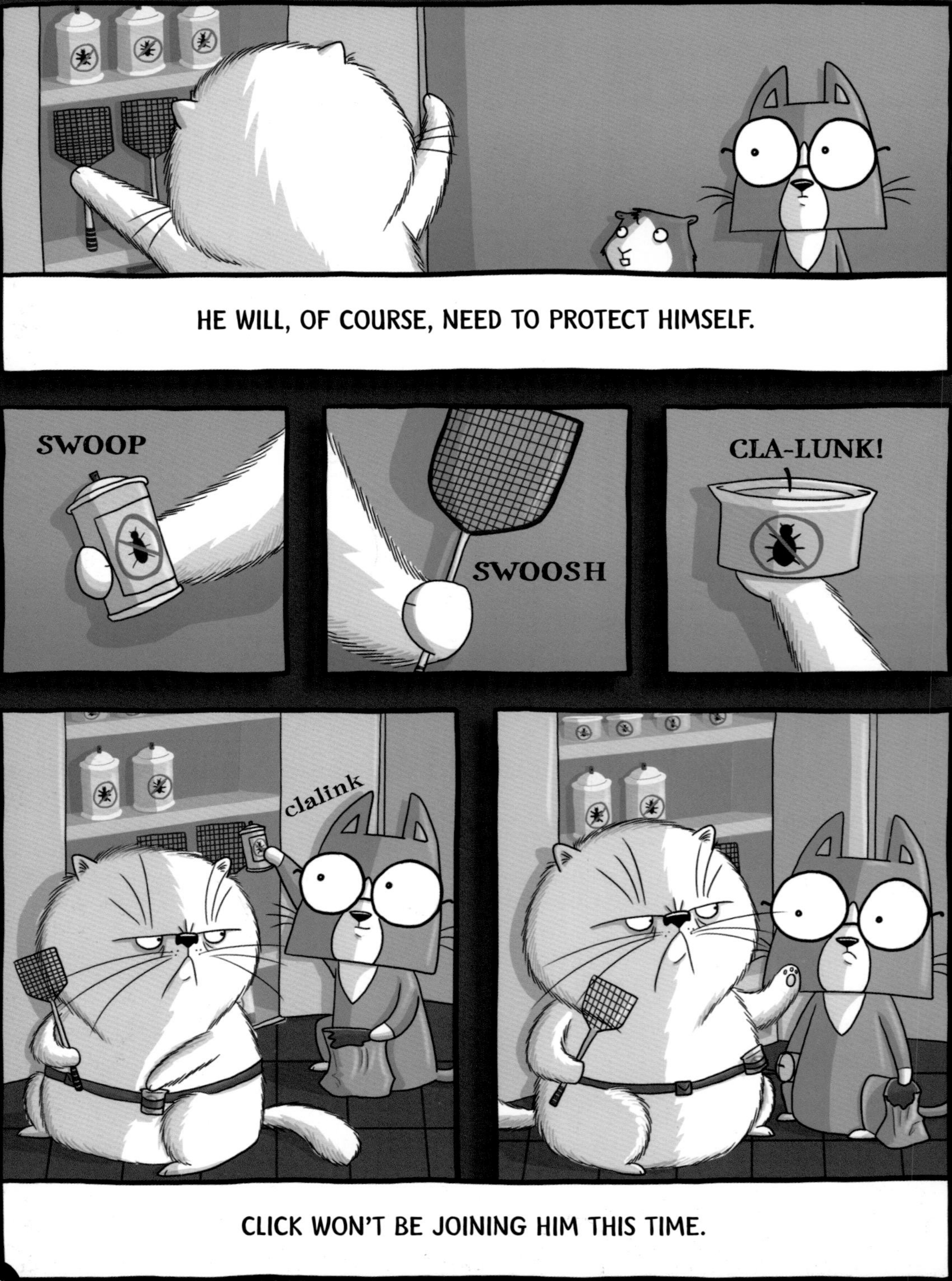
HE WILL, OF COURSE, NEED TO PROTECT HIMSELF.
SWOOP
SWOOSH
CLA-LUNK!
clalink
CLICK WON'T BE JOINING HIM THIS TIME.

HE WON'T PUT HER IN THAT KIND OF DANGER.

THIS WILL BE A SOLO MISSION.

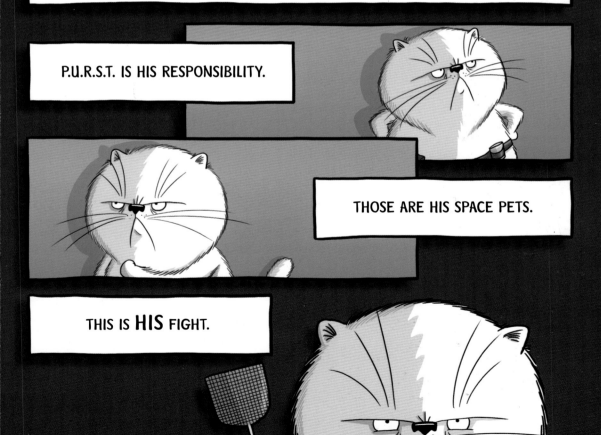

P.U.R.S.T. IS HIS RESPONSIBILITY.

THOSE ARE HIS SPACE PETS.

THIS IS **HIS** FIGHT.

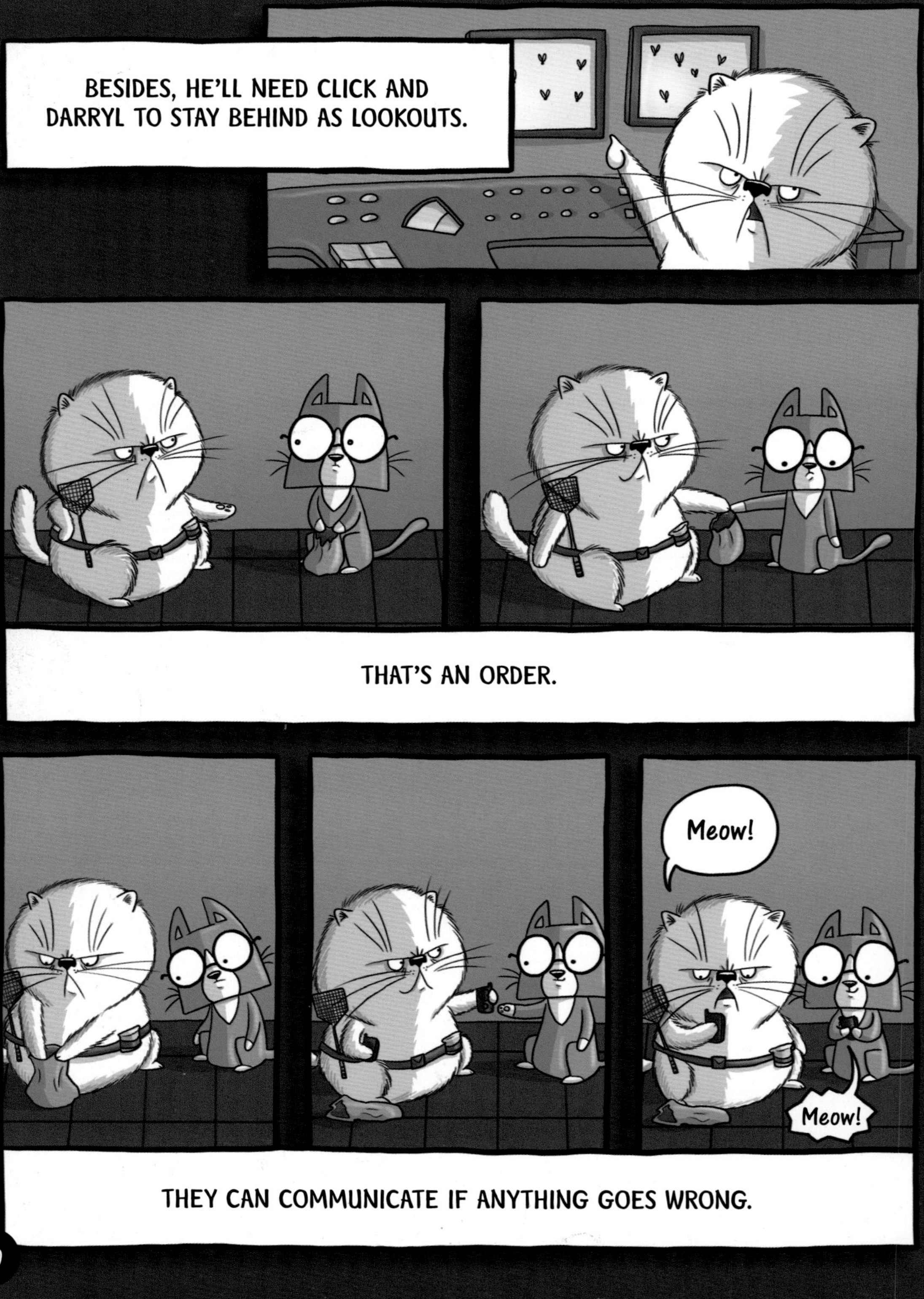
BESIDES, HE'LL NEED CLICK AND DARRYL TO STAY BEHIND AS LOOKOUTS.
THAT'S AN ORDER.
Meow!
Meow!
THEY CAN COMMUNICATE IF ANYTHING GOES WRONG.

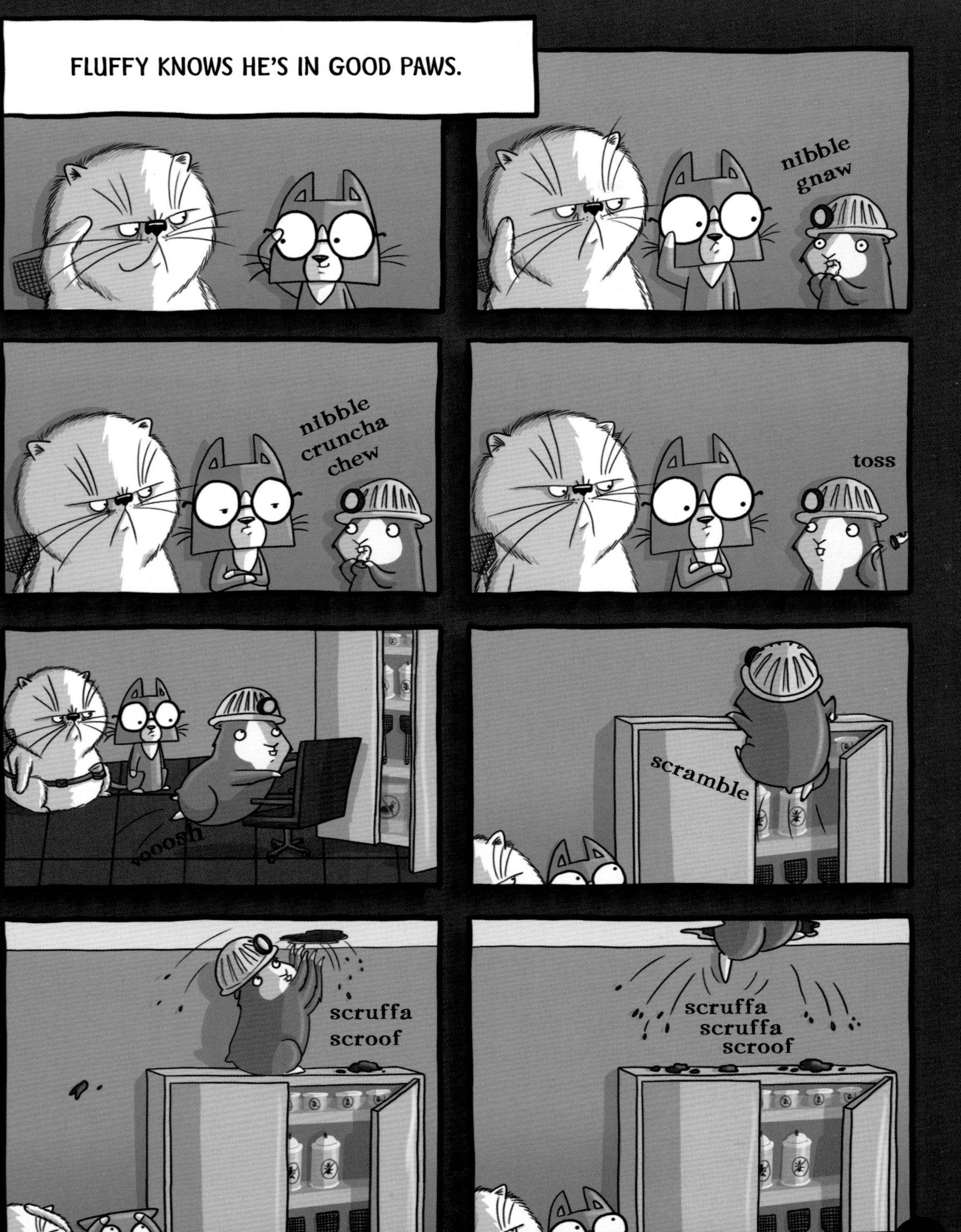
FLUFFY KNOWS HE'S IN GOOD PAWS.
nibble
gnaw
nibble
cruncha
chew
toss
scramble
scruffa
scroof
scruffa
scruffa
scroof

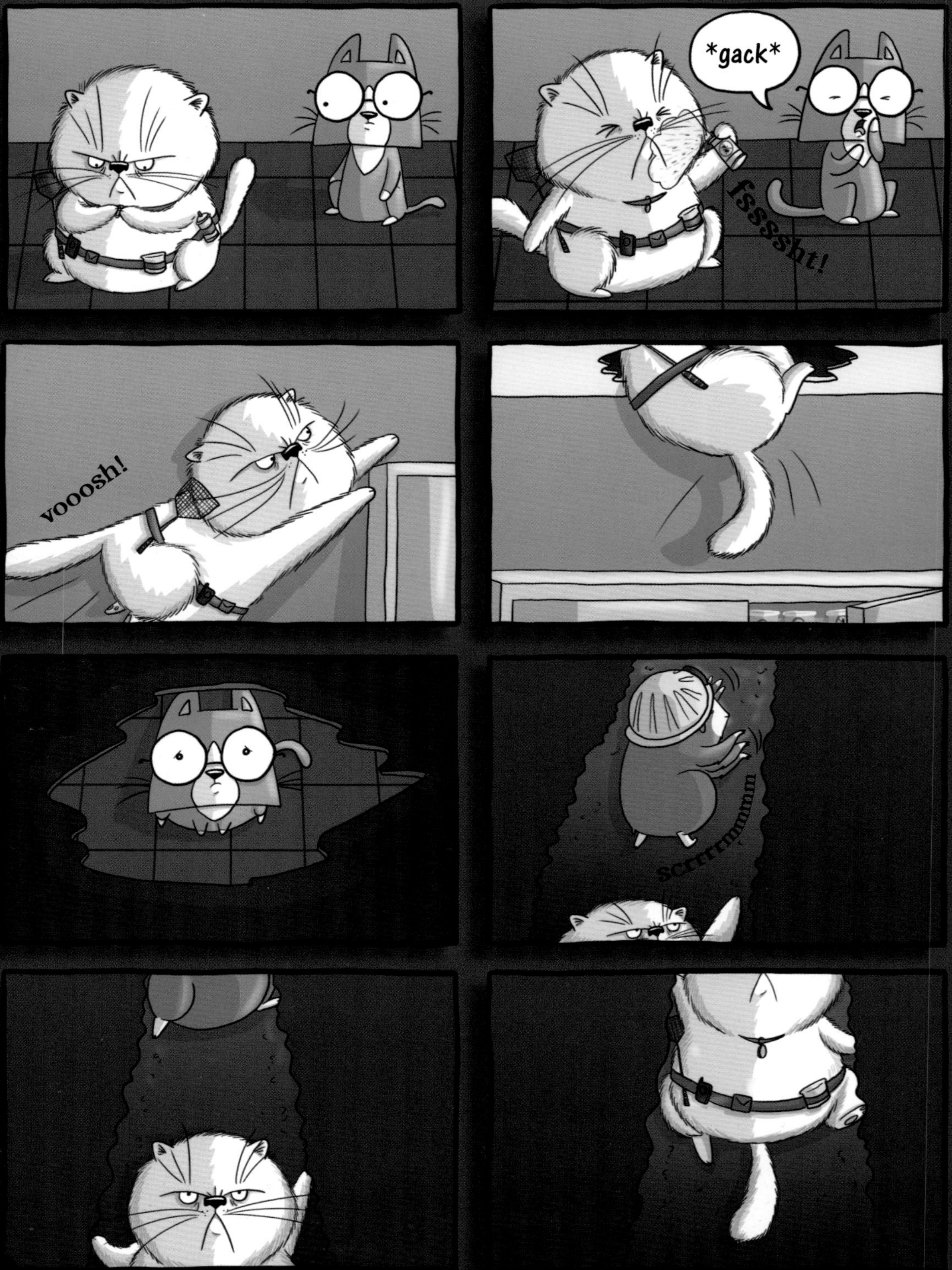
gack
fsssssht!
vooosh!
scrrrrmmmmm

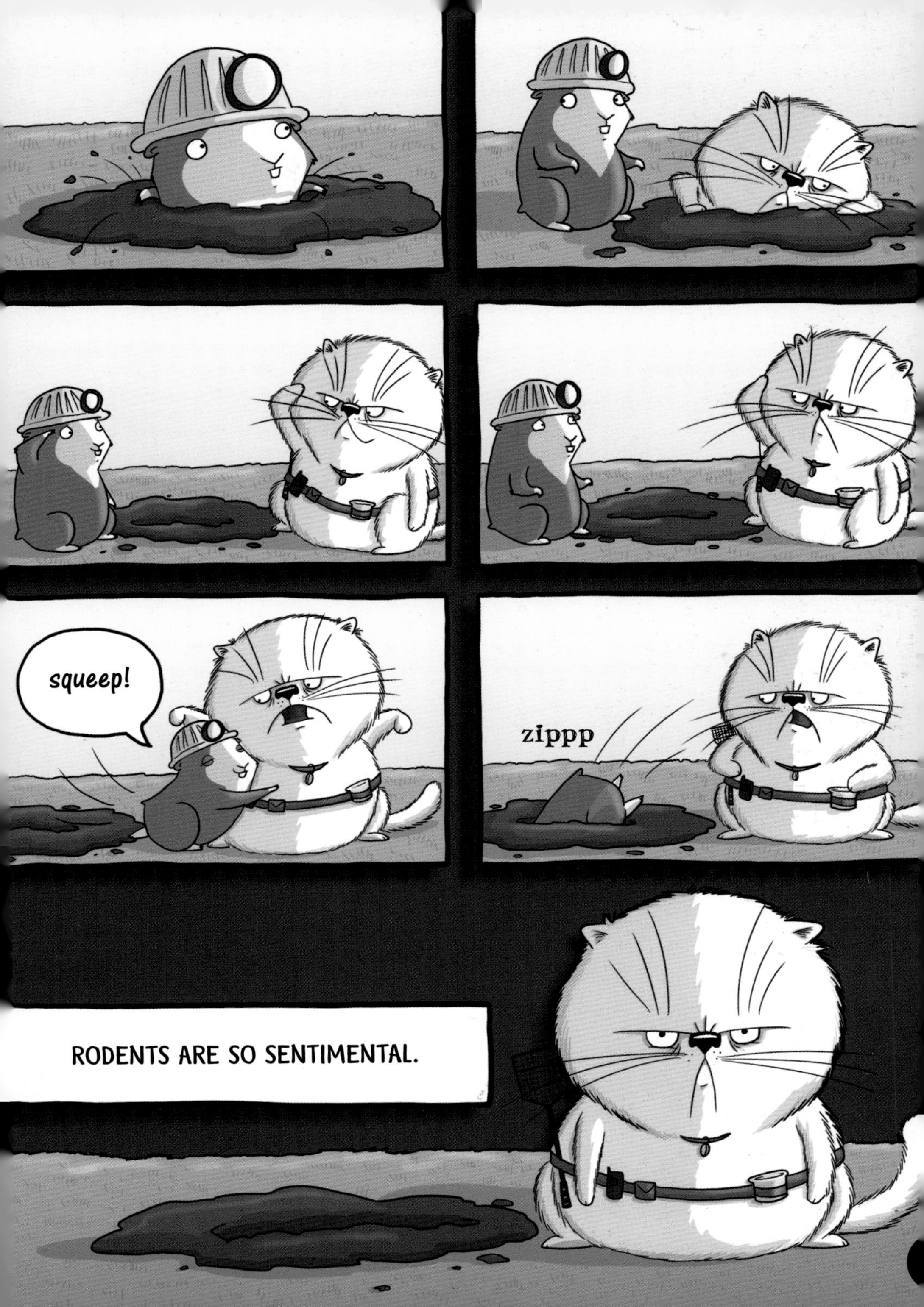
squeep!
zippp
RODENTS ARE SO SENTIMENTAL.

AFTER ALL THESE QUIET YEARS, SERGEANT FLUFFY VANDERMERE IS A CAT OF ACTION ONCE MORE.

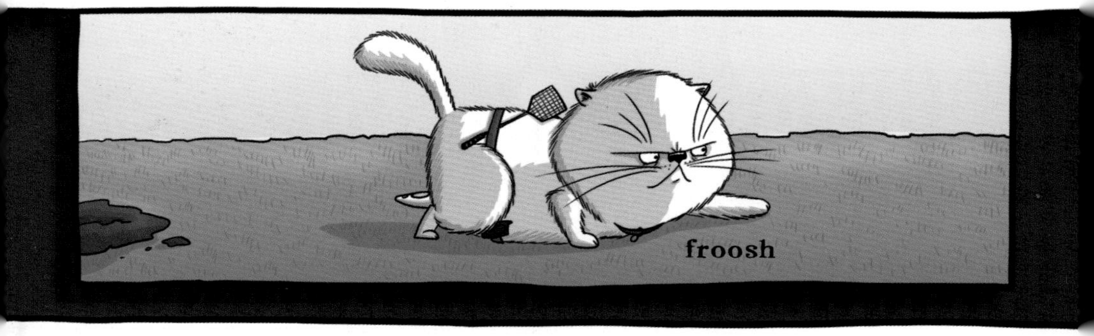
froosh

TIME TO GET DOWN TO BUSINESS.

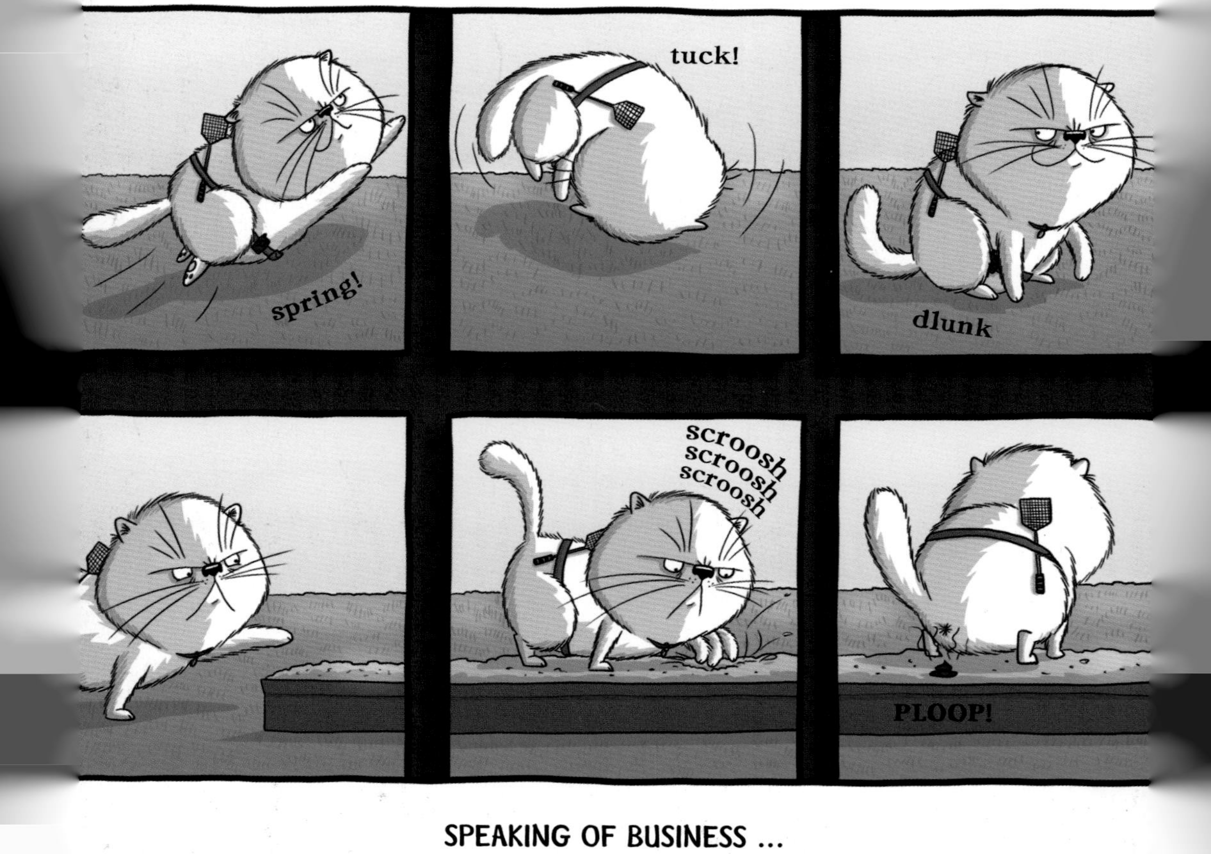
spring!
tuck!
dlunk
scroosh
scroosh
scroosh
PLOOP!

SPEAKING OF BUSINESS ...

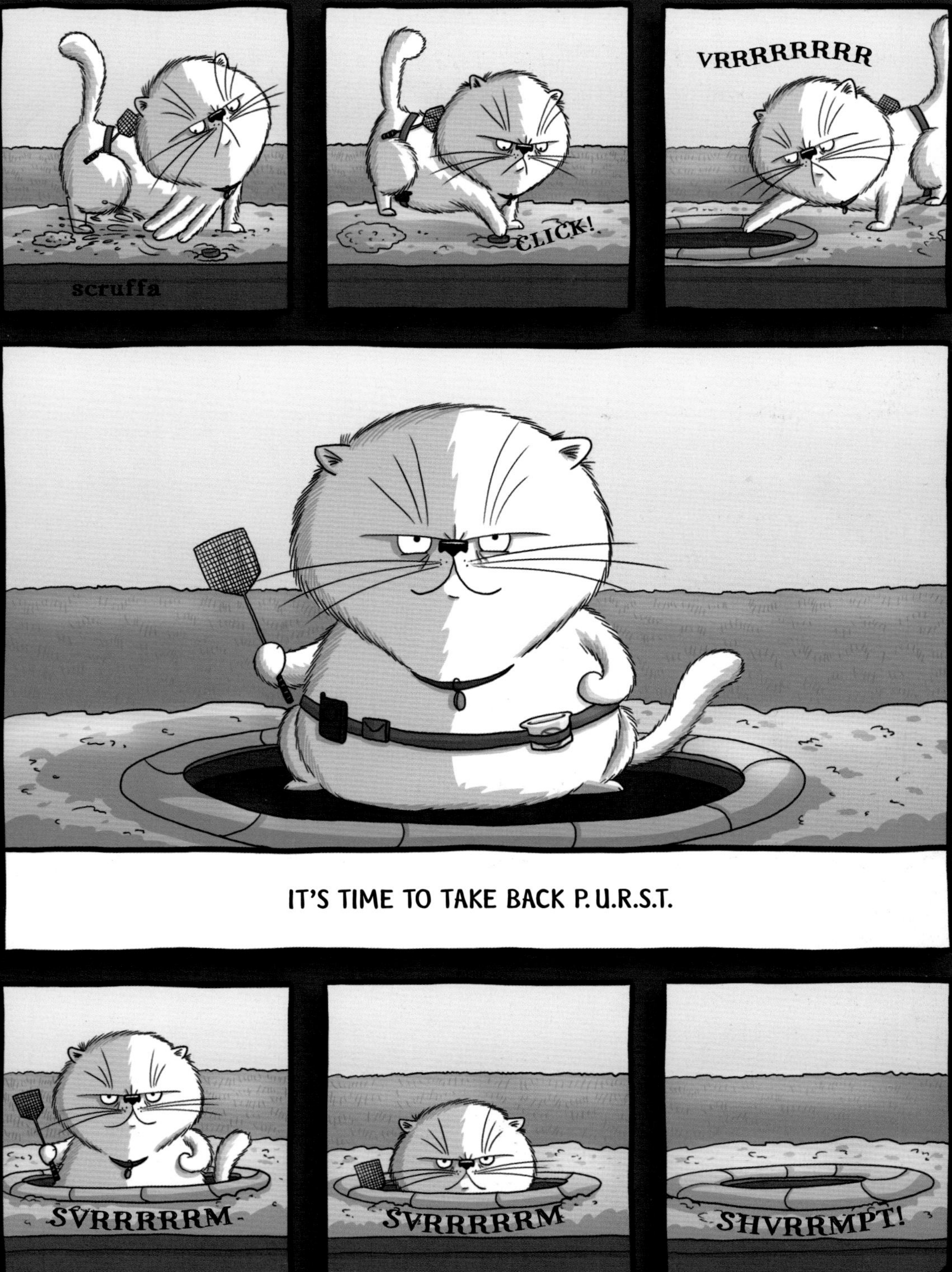
scruffa
CLICK!
VRRRRRRRR
IT'S TIME TO TAKE BACK P.U.R.S.T.
SVRRRRRRM
SVRRRRRRM
SHVRRMPT!

LEVEL ONE ...

IT'S QUIET.

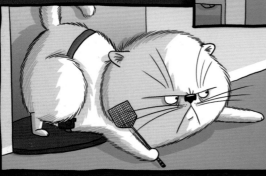

FLUFFY CAN BE QUIET, TOO.

bzzzz

bzzzzzzz

bzzzzzzzzzzz

HEEERE'S FLUFFY!

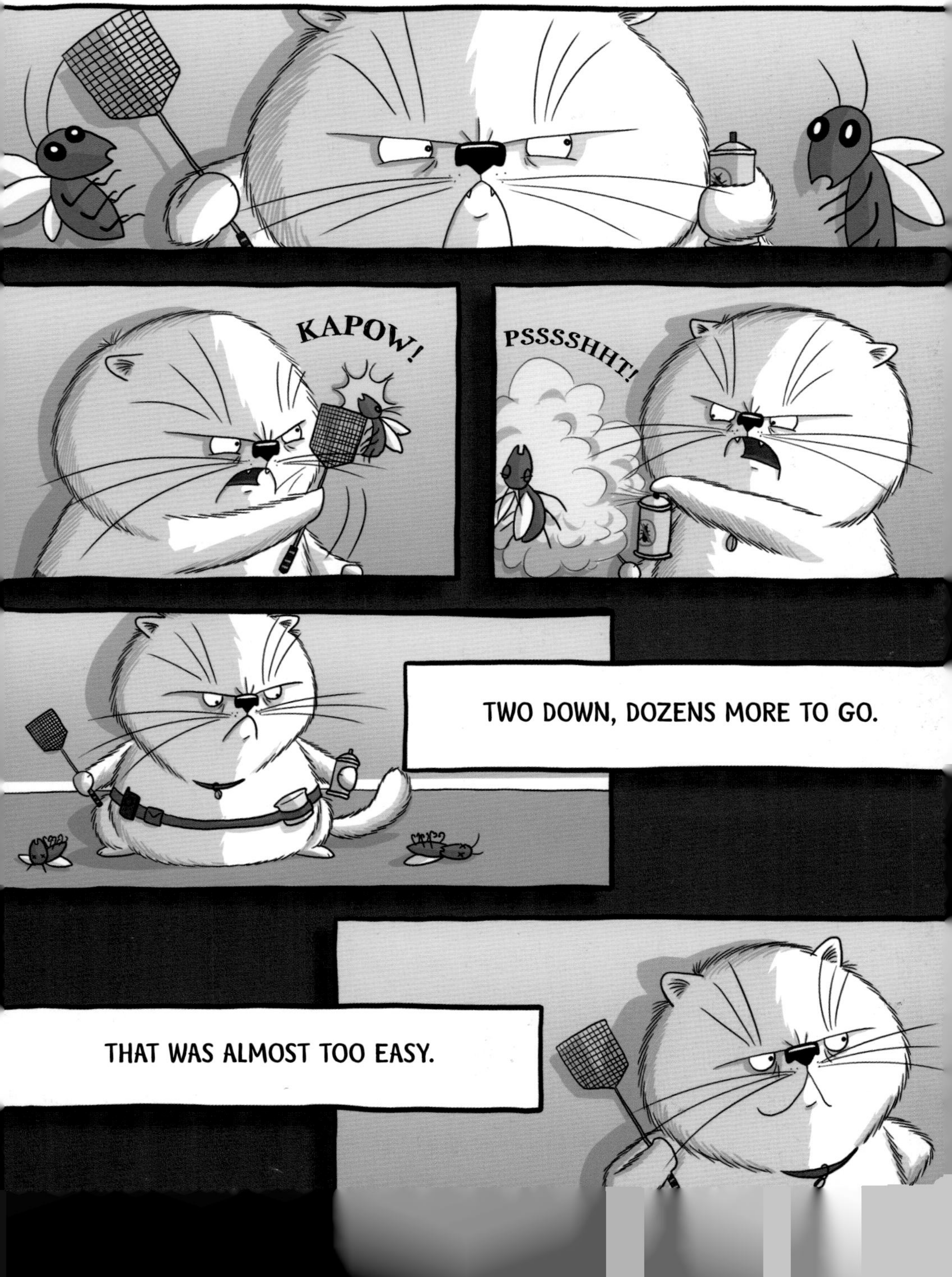
KAPOW!
PSSSSHHT!
TWO DOWN, DOZENS MORE TO GO.
THAT WAS ALMOST TOO EASY.

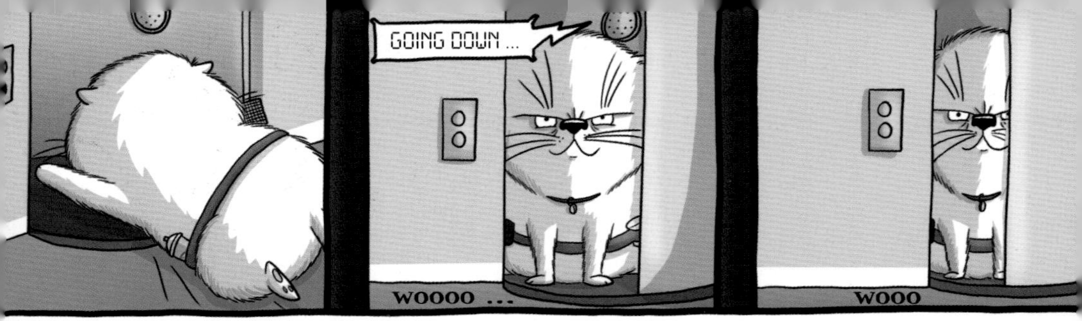
GOING DOWN ...
WOOOO ...
WOOO

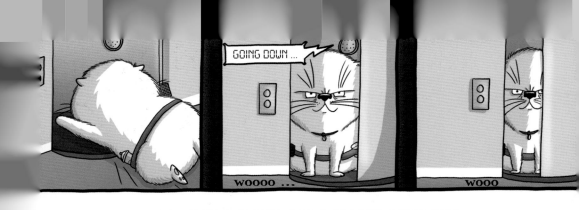

FLUFFY WAS HOPING FOR A BIGGER CHALLENGE.

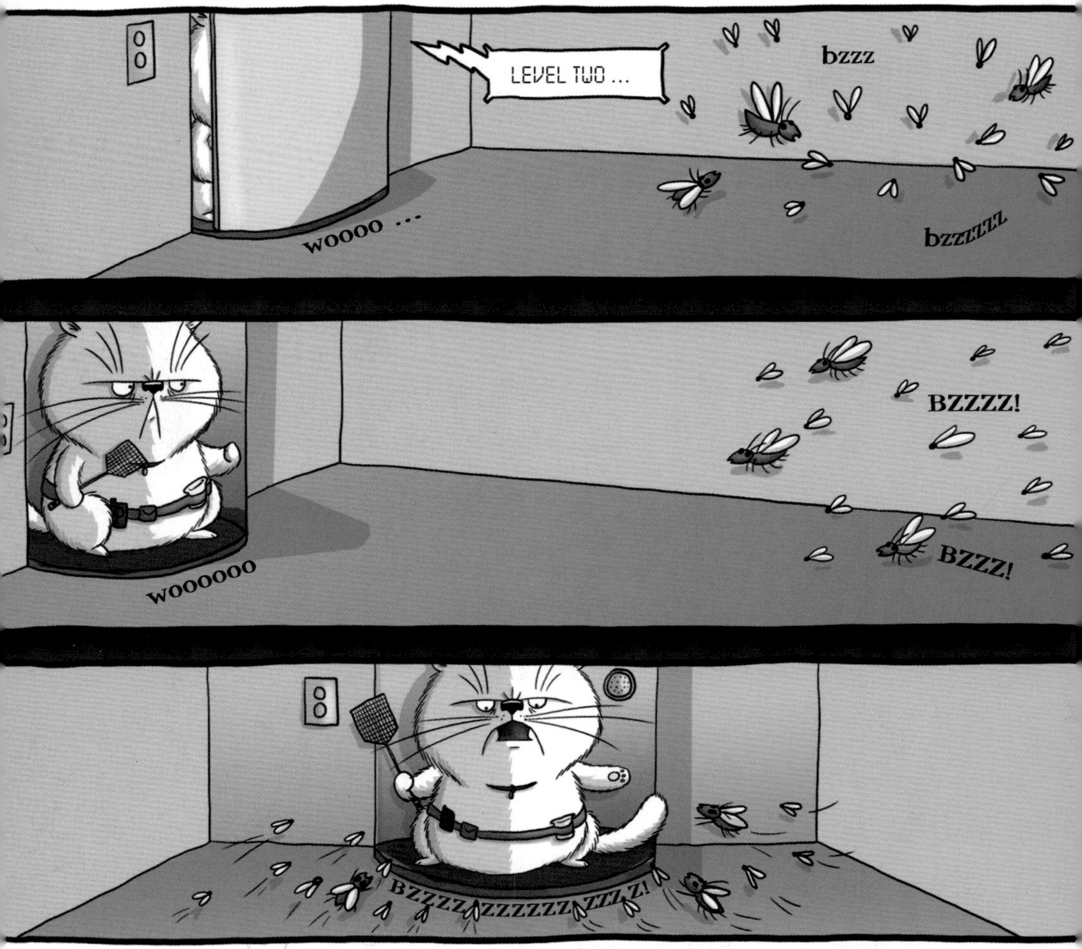
LEVEL TWO ...
bzzz
WOOOO ...
bzzzzzz
BZZZZ!
BZZZ!
WOOOOOO

HE SHOULD BE CAREFUL WHAT HE WISHES FOR.

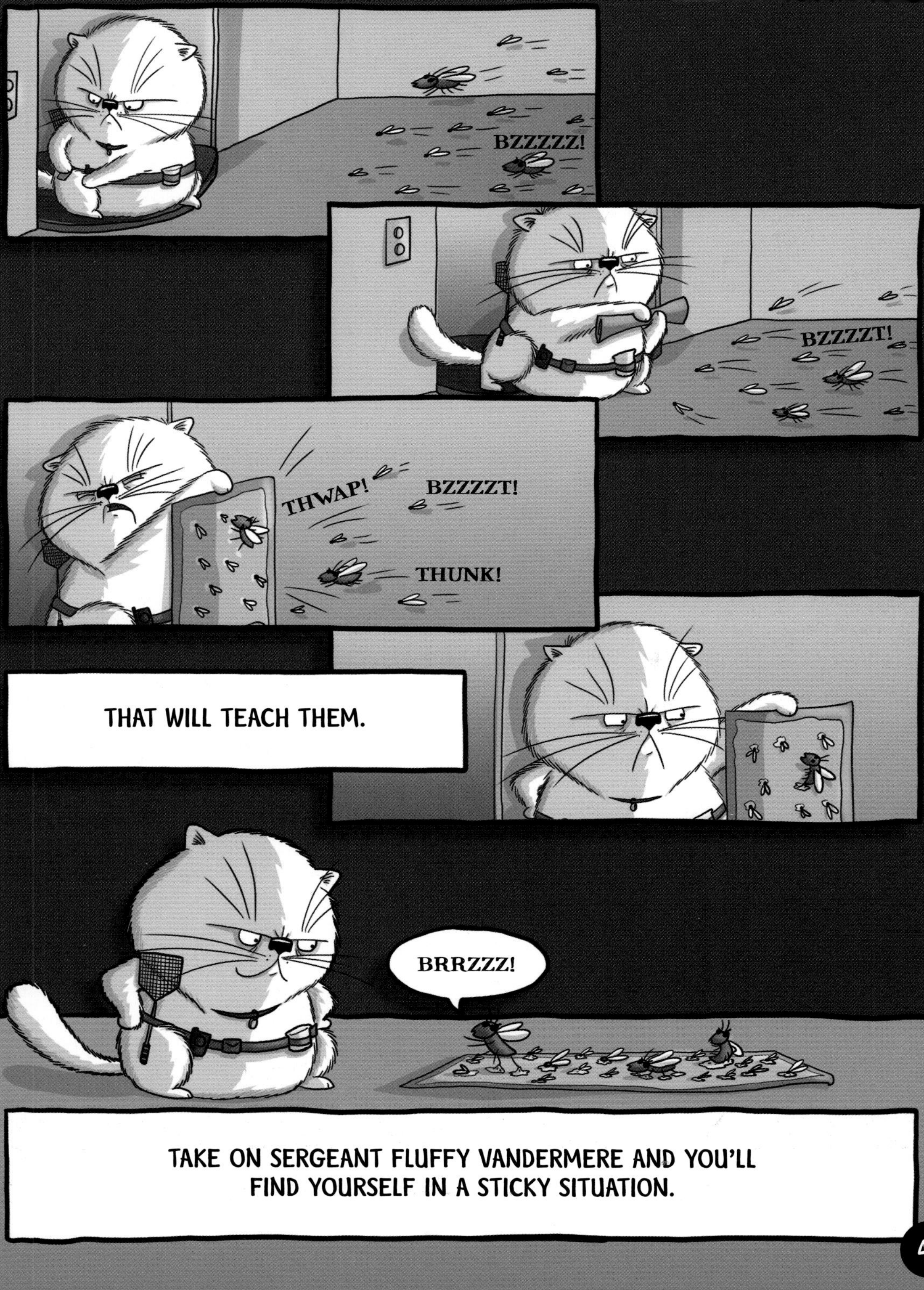
BZZZZZ!
BZZZZT!
THWAP!
BZZZZT!
THUNK!
THAT WILL TEACH THEM.
BRRZZZ!
TAKE ON SERGEANT FLUFFY VANDERMERE AND YOU'LL FIND YOURSELF IN A STICKY SITUATION.

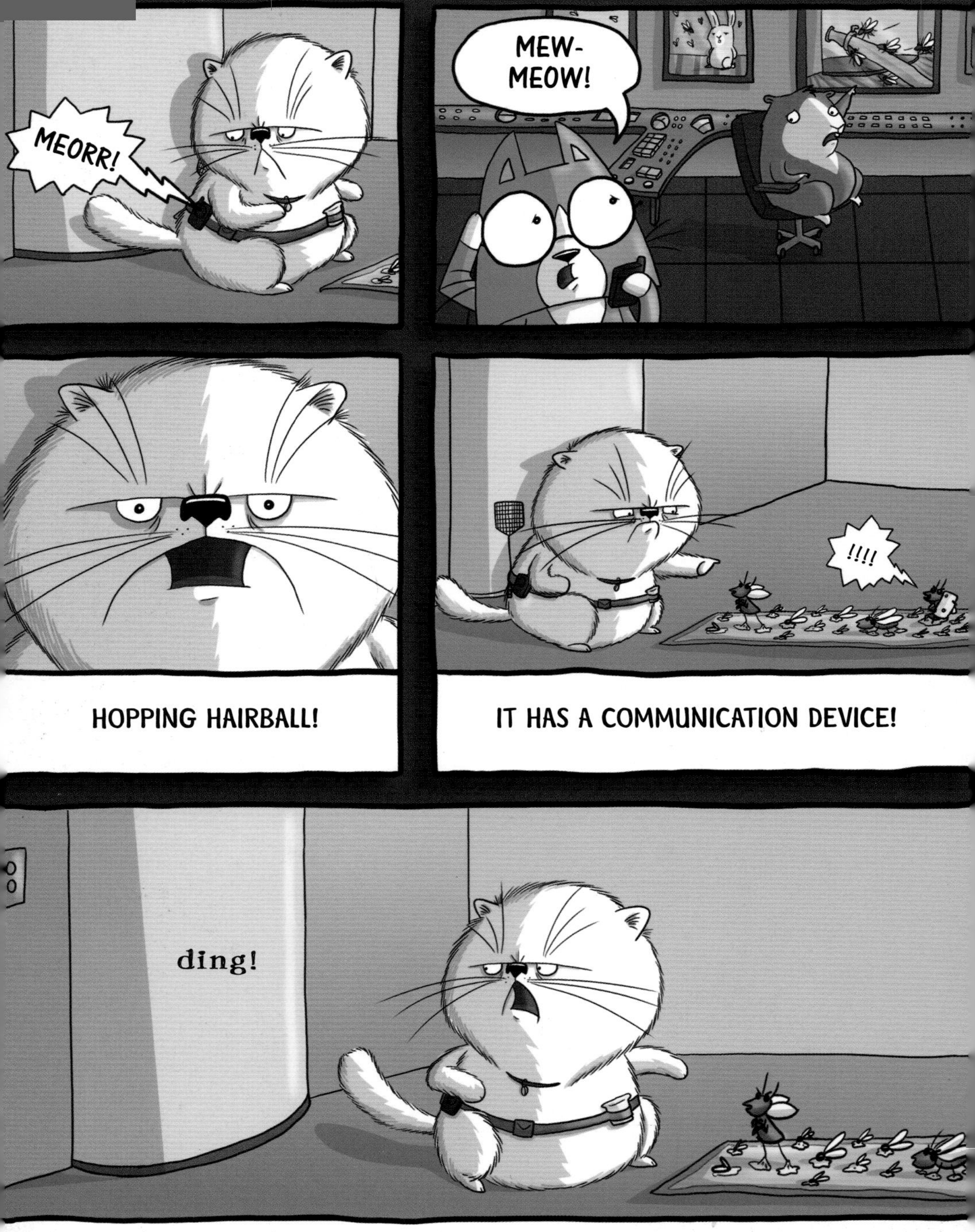
MEORR!
MEW-MEOW!
HOPPING HAIRBALL!
!!!!
IT HAS A COMMUNICATION DEVICE!
ding!

THE OTHER ALIENS ARE COMING FOR HIM!

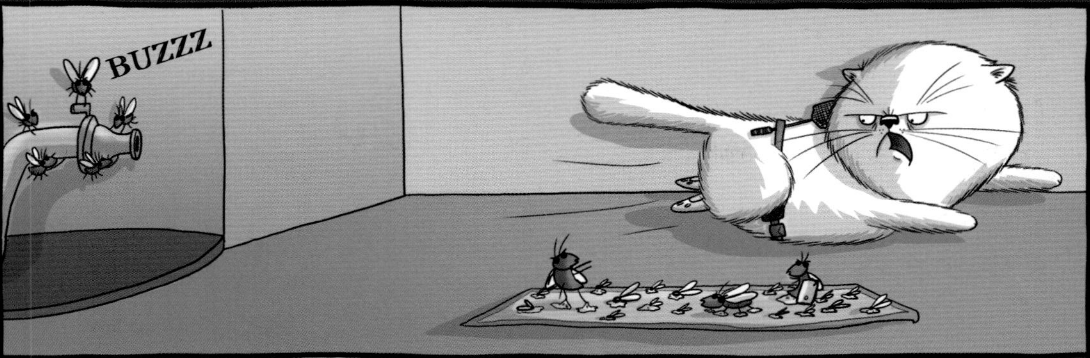
BUZZZ

HE'LL HAVE TO FIND ANOTHER WAY TO THE CADETS.

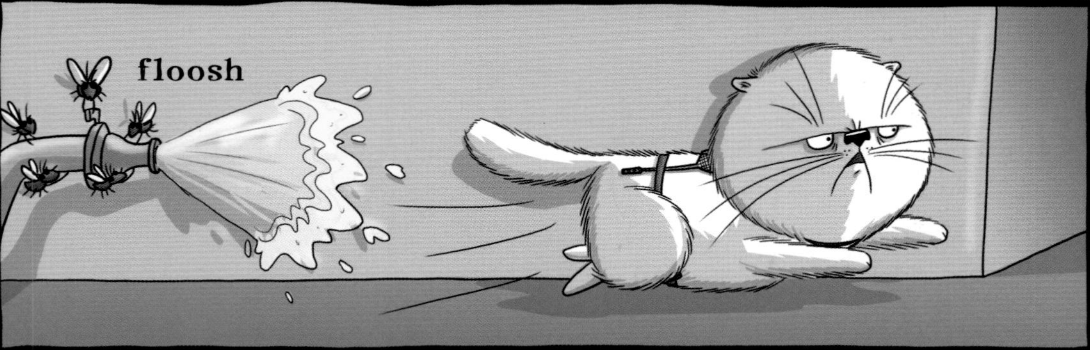
floosh

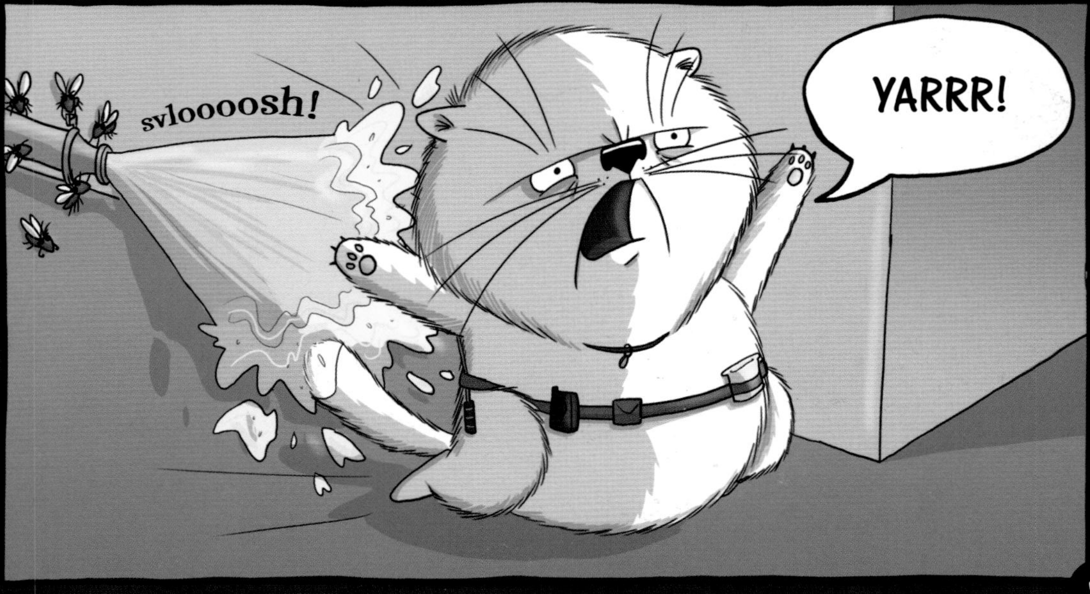
svlooooosh!
YARRR!

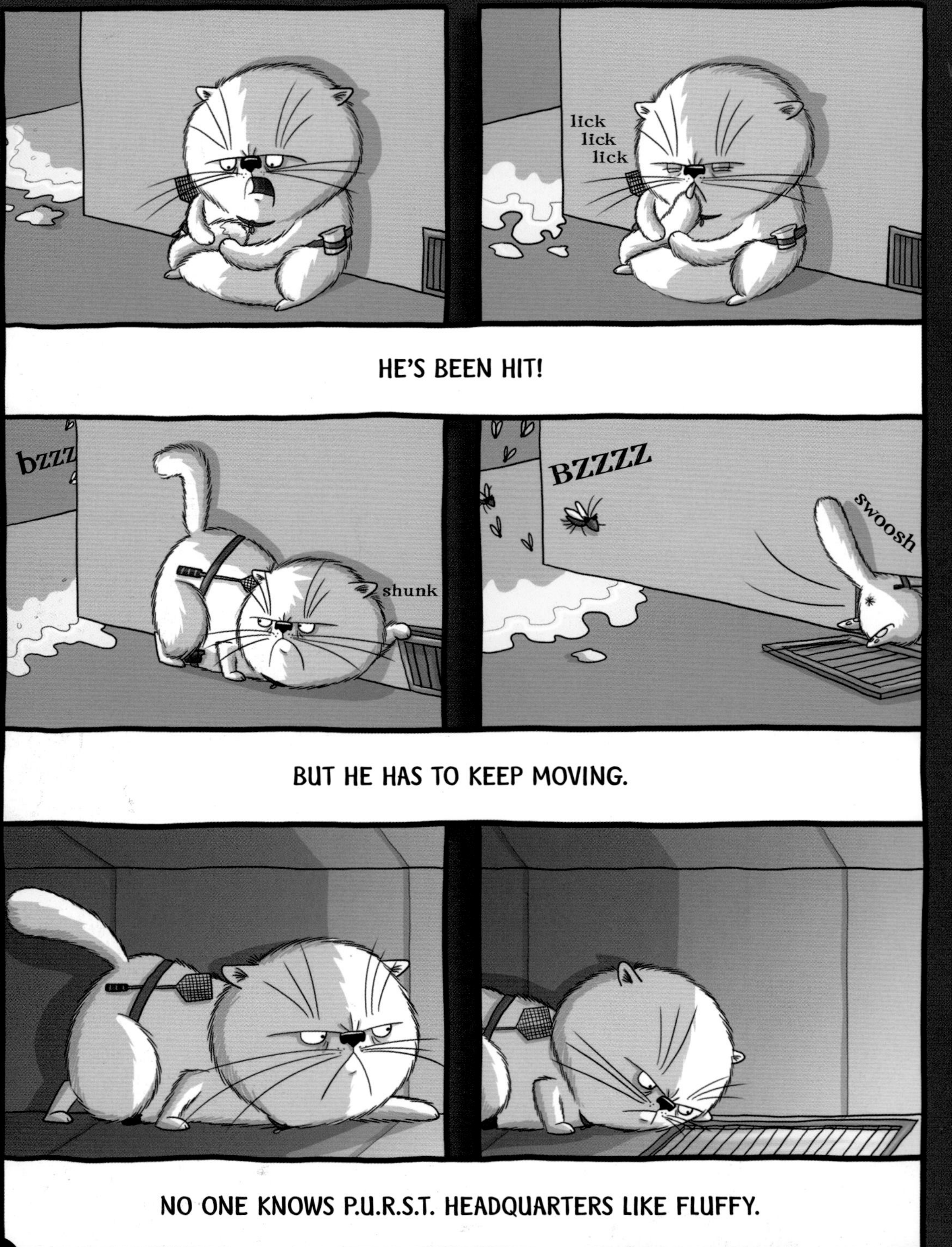
lick
lick
lick
HE'S BEEN HIT!
bzzz
shunk
BZZZZ
swoosh
BUT HE HAS TO KEEP MOVING.
NO ONE KNOWS P.U.R.S.T. HEADQUARTERS LIKE FLUFFY.

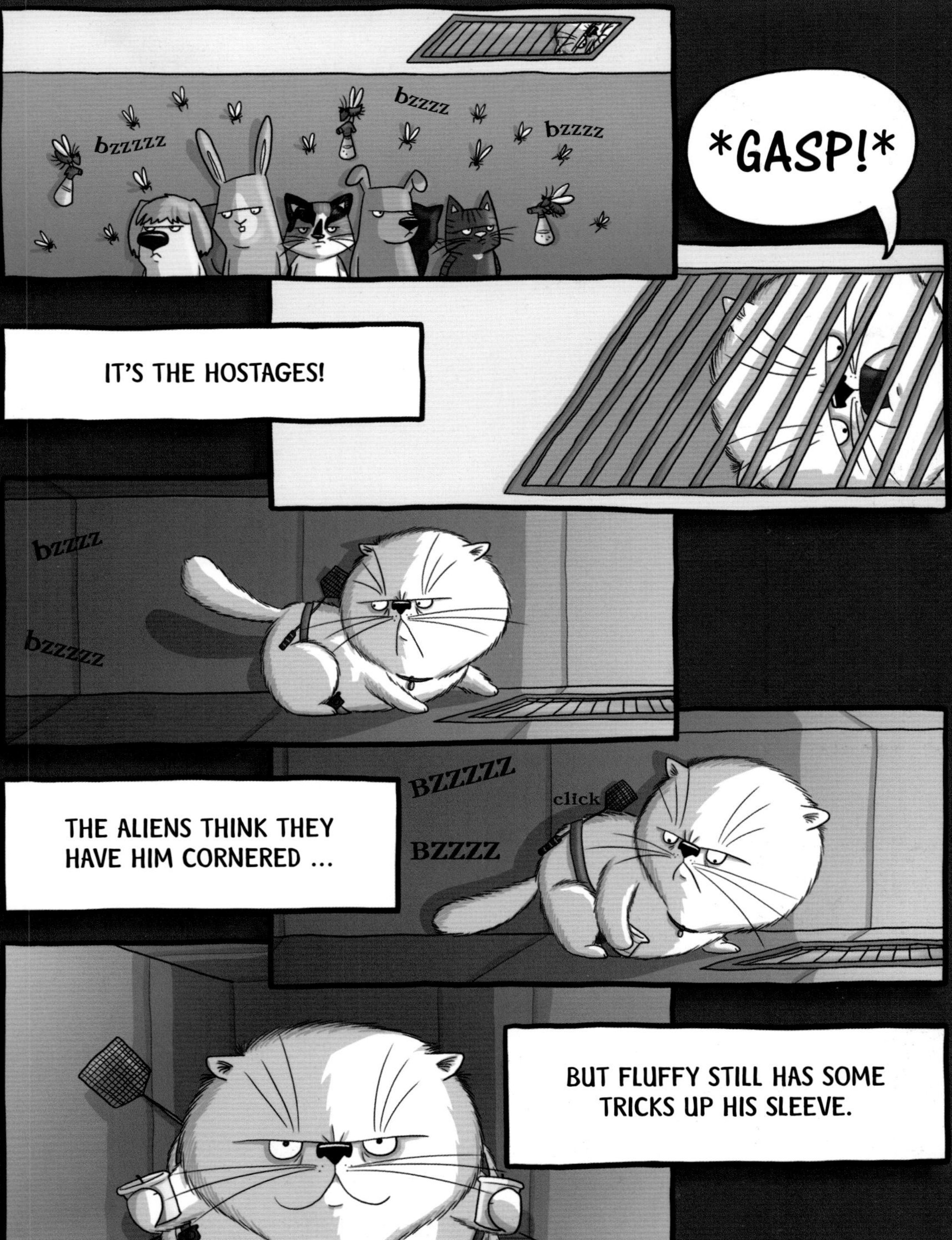
bzzzzz
bzzzz
bzzzz
GASP!
IT'S THE HOSTAGES!
bzzzz
bzzzzz
BZZZZZ
click
BZZZZ
THE ALIENS THINK THEY HAVE HIM CORNERED ...
BUT FLUFFY STILL HAS SOME TRICKS UP HIS SLEEVE.

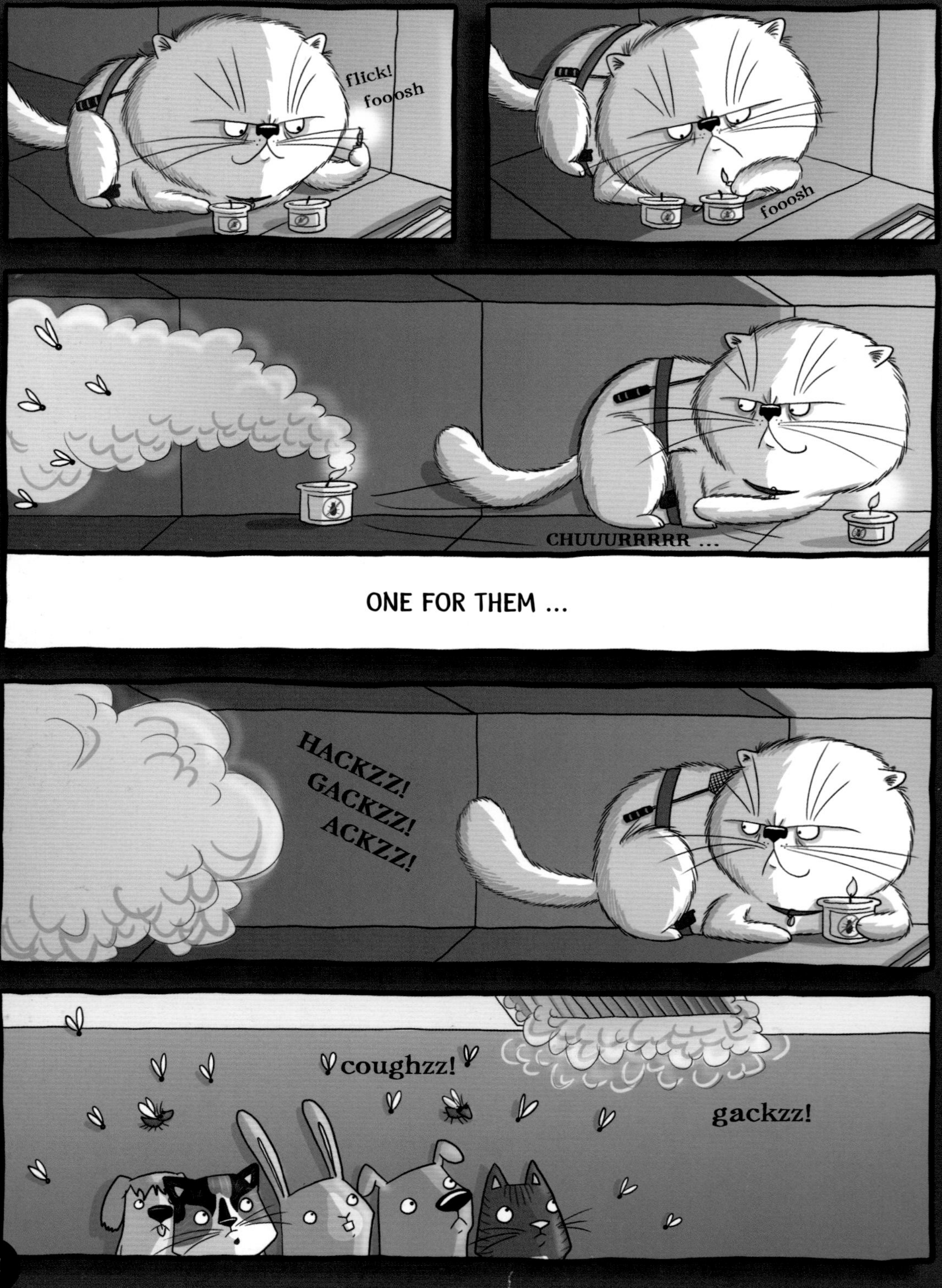
flick!
fooosh
fooosh
CHUUURRRRR ...
ONE FOR THEM ...
HACKZZ!
GACKZZ!
ACKZZ!
coughzz!
gackzz!

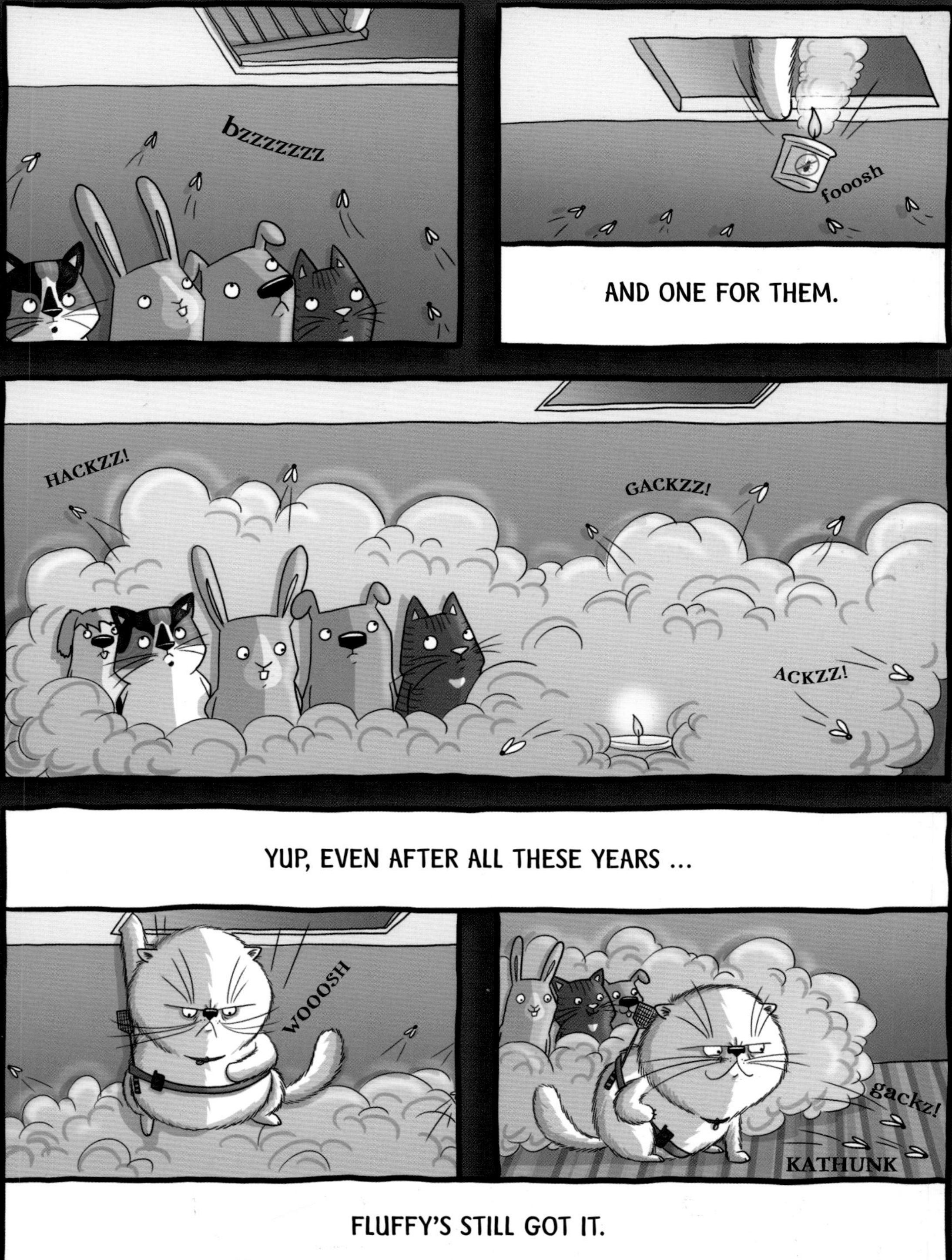
bzzzzzzz
fooosh
AND ONE FOR THEM.
HACKZZ!
GACKZZ!
ACKZZ!
YUP, EVEN AFTER ALL THESE YEARS ...
WOOOSH
gackz!
KATHUNK
FLUFFY'S STILL GOT IT.

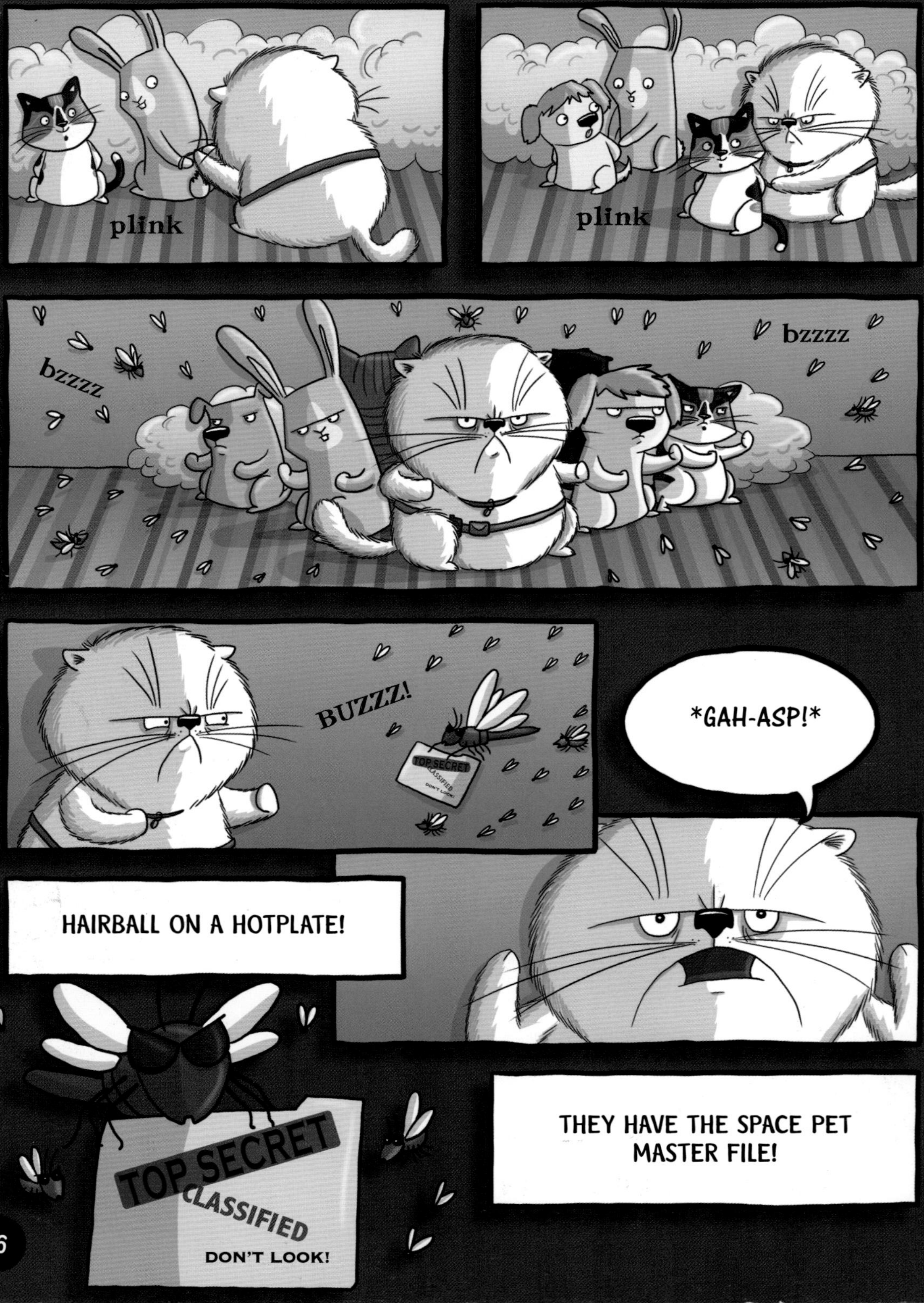
plink
plink
bzzzz
bzzzz
BUZZZ!
TOP SECRET
CLASSIFIED
DON'T LOOK!
GAH-ASP!
HAIRBALL ON A HOTPLATE!
THEY HAVE THE SPACE PET MASTER FILE!
TOP SECRET
CLASSIFIED
DON'T LOOK!

THAT'S WHAT THE ATTACK WAS ALL ABOUT!

THE ALIENS WANT TO STEAL THE NAMES AND LOCATIONS ...

bzzzz!

OF EVERY SPACE PET AND SPACE STATION IN THE WORLD.

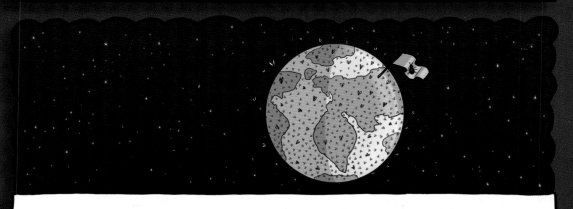

WITH THAT KNOWLEDGE, ALIENS COULD WIPE OUT P.U.R.S.T. FOREVER!

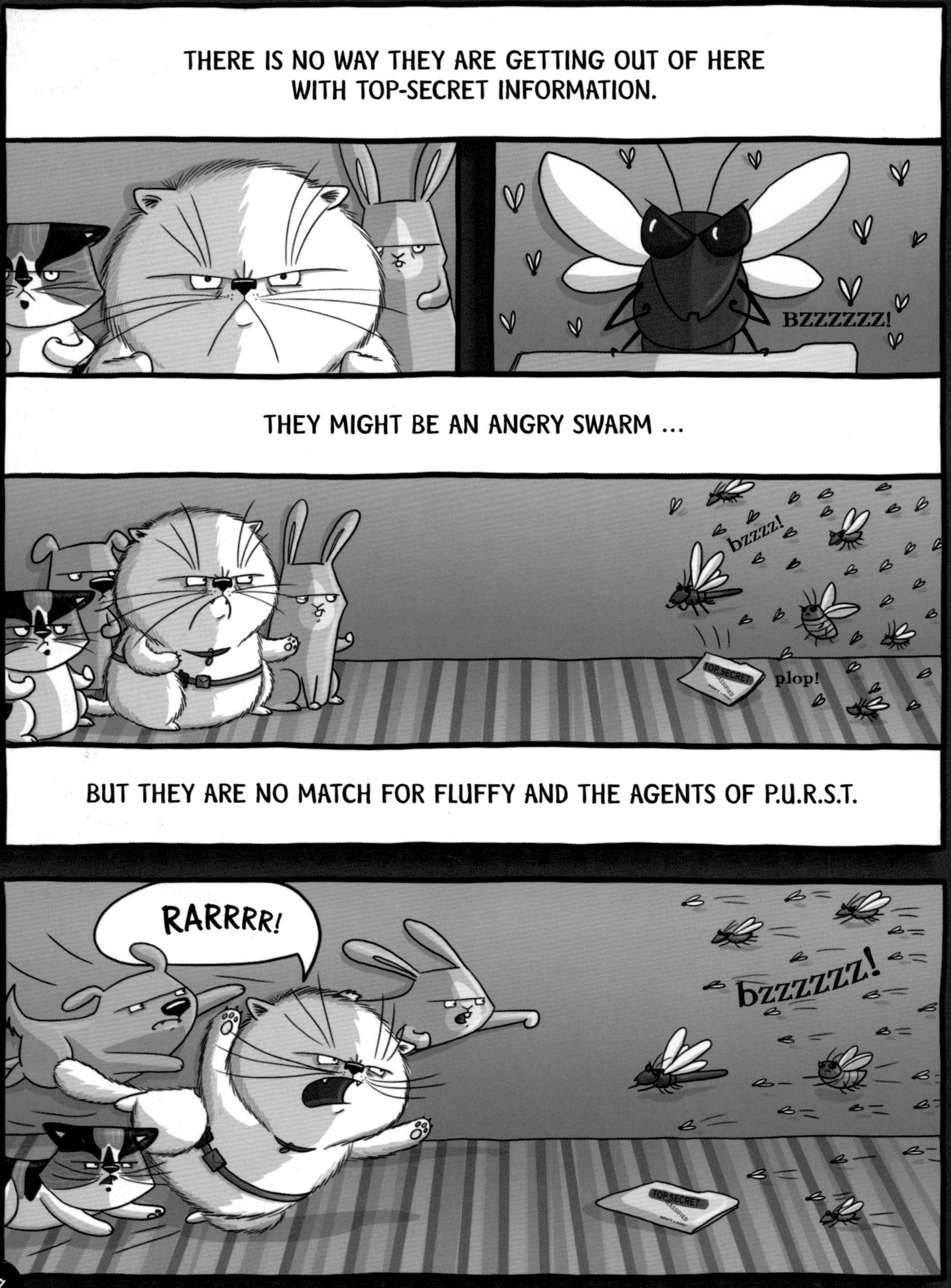
THERE IS NO WAY THEY ARE GETTING OUT OF HERE WITH TOP-SECRET INFORMATION.
BZZZZZZ!
THEY MIGHT BE AN ANGRY SWARM ...
bzzzz!
TOP SECRET
plop!
BUT THEY ARE NO MATCH FOR FLUFFY AND THE AGENTS OF P.U.R.S.T.
RARRRR!
bzzzzzz!
TOP SECRET

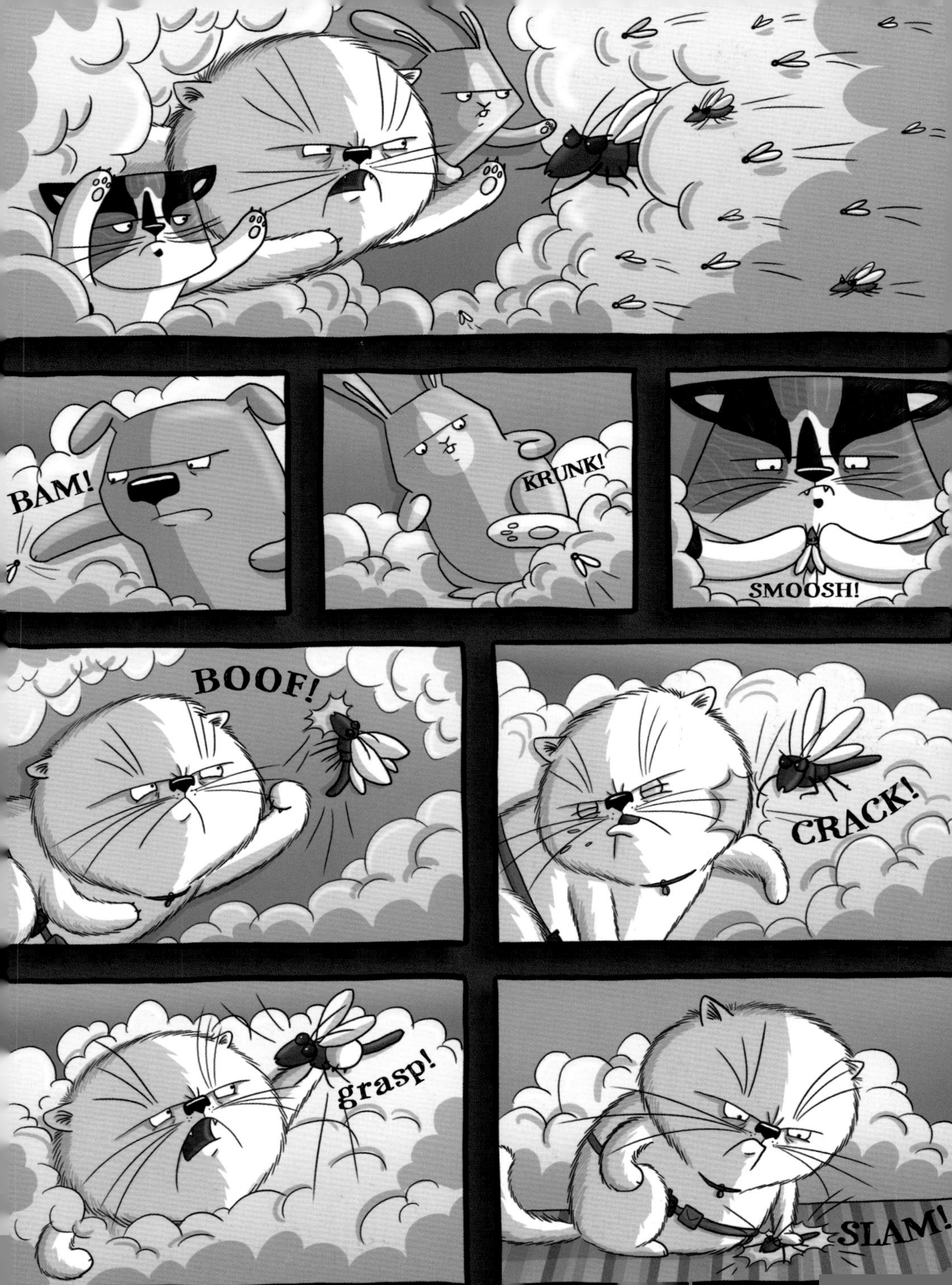
BAM!
KRUNK!
SMOOSH!
BOOF!
CRACK!
grasp!
SLAM!

NICE TRY, BUT NO ONE CAN DEFEAT P.U.R.S.T.

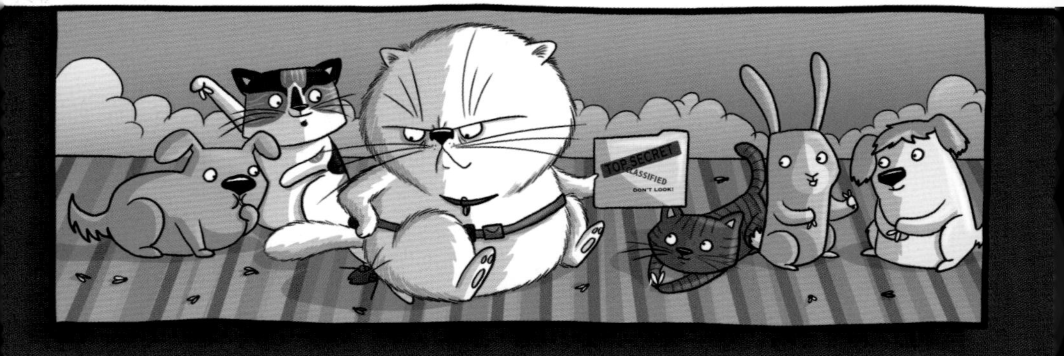
TOP SECRET
DON'T LOOK!

P.U.R.S.T. HEADQUARTERS IS SECURE.

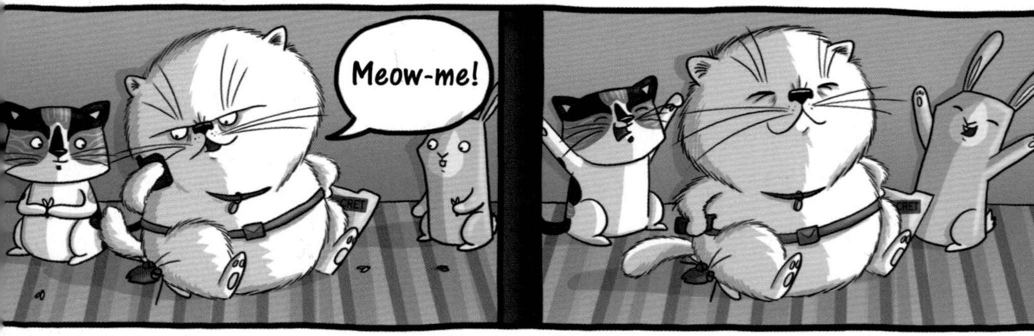
Meow-me!

HE NOTIFIES CLICK AND DARRYL.

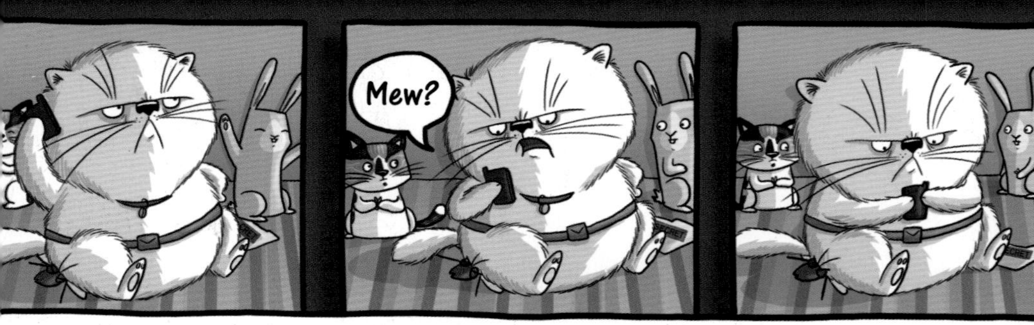
Mew?

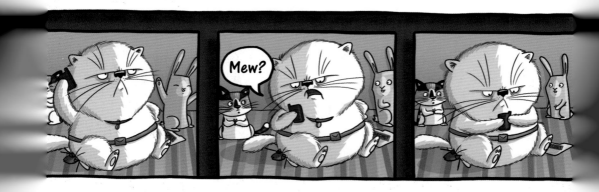

CLICK? DARRYL? NO ANSWER. THAT'S STRANGE.

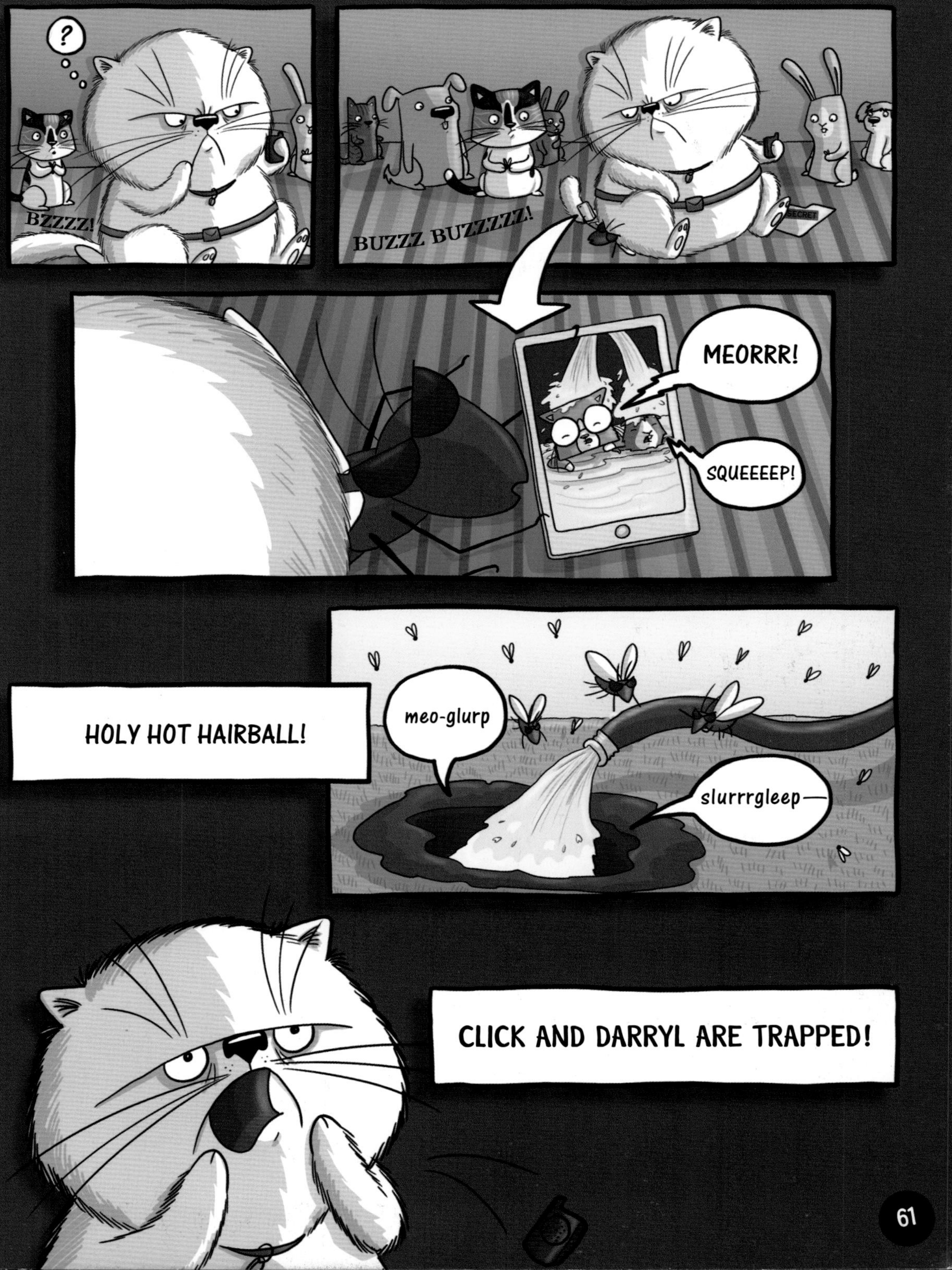

?
BZZZZ!
BUZZZ BUZZZZZ!
SECRET
MEORRR!
SQUEEEEP!
HOLY HOT HAIRBALL!
meo-glurp
slurrrgleep—
CLICK AND DARRYL ARE TRAPPED!

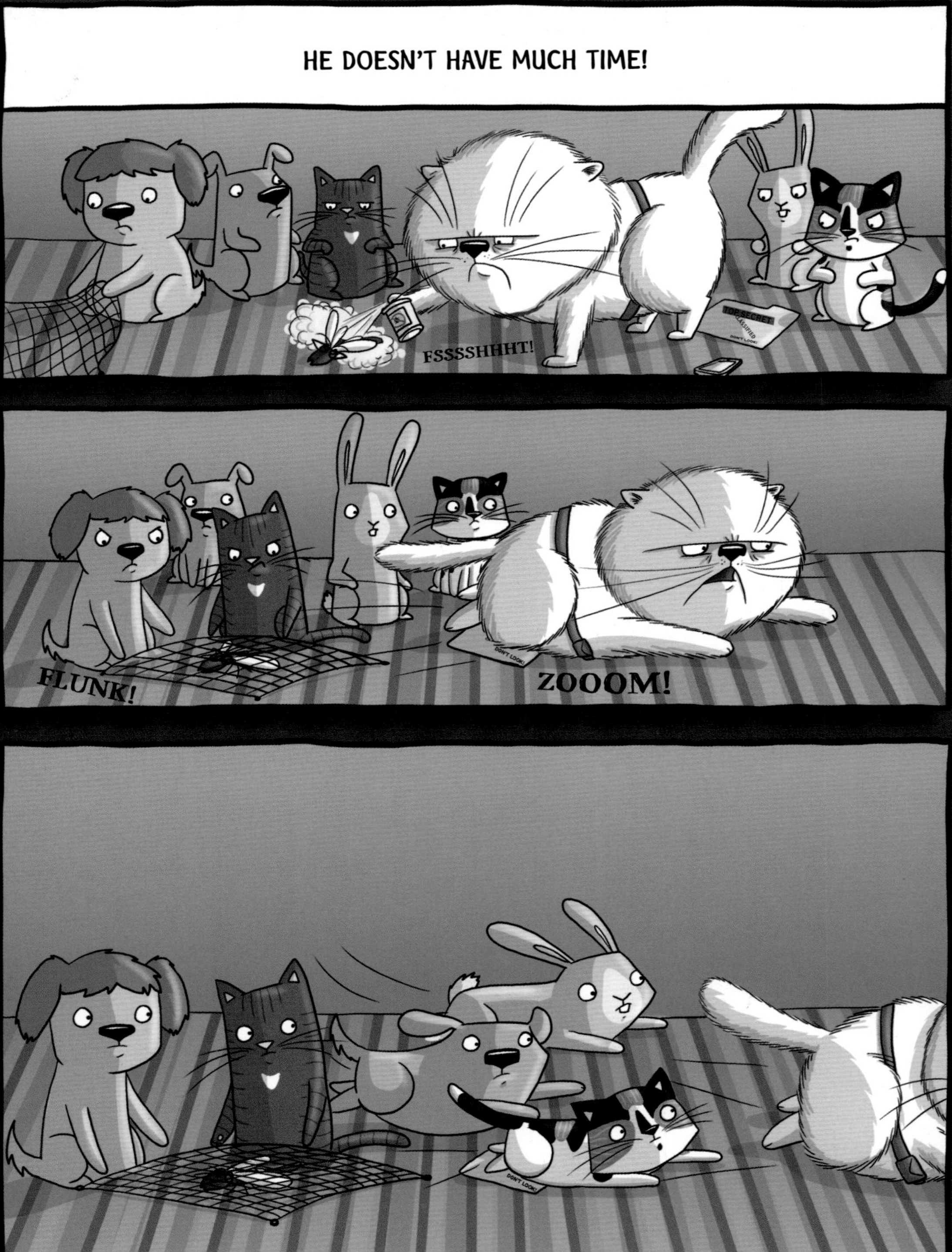
HE DOESN'T HAVE MUCH TIME!
TOP SECRET
CLASSIFIED
DON'T LOOK!
FSSSSHHHT!
FLUNK!
DON'T LOOK!
ZOOOM!
DON'T LOOK!

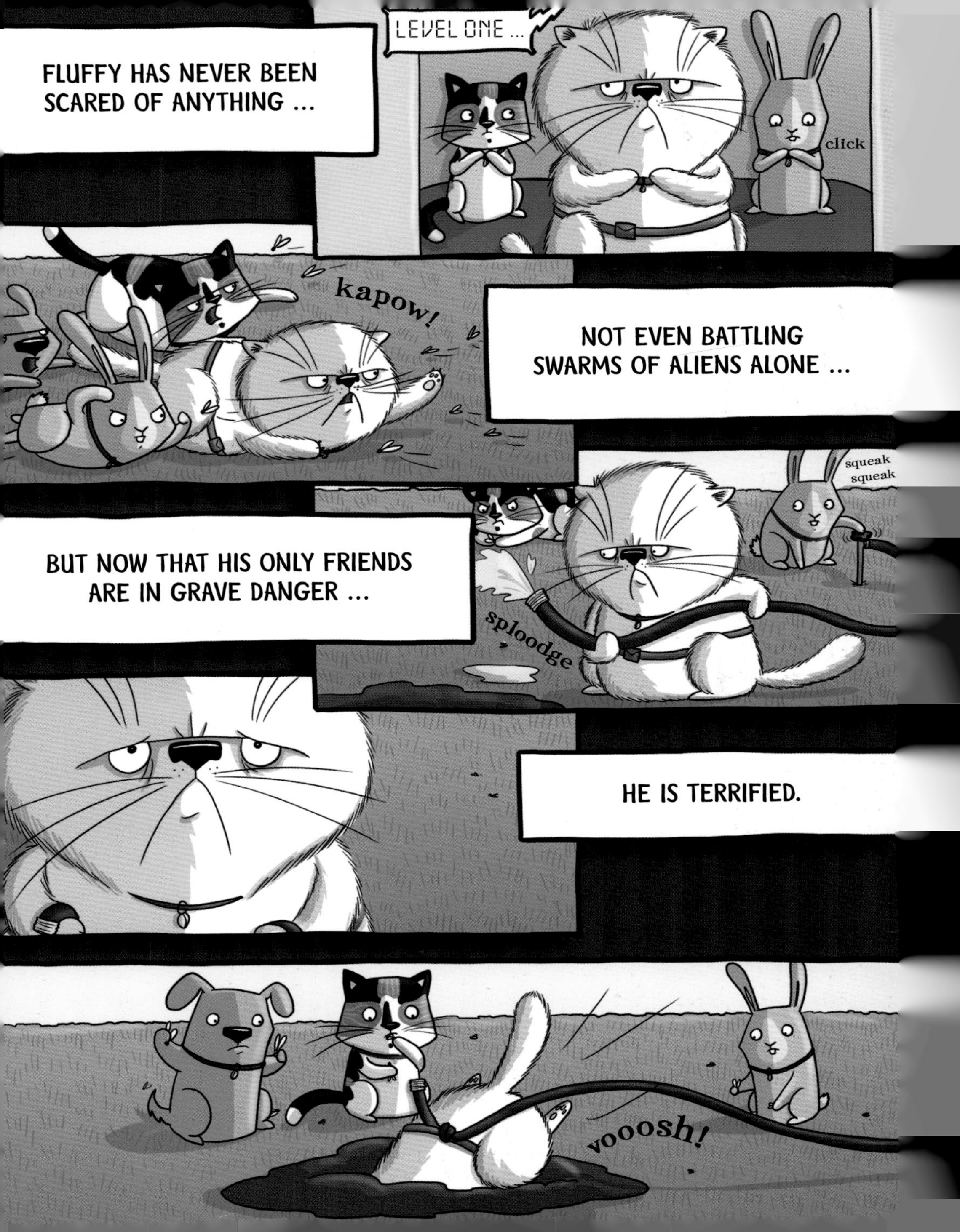
FLUFFY HAS NEVER BEEN SCARED OF ANYTHING ...
LEVEL ONE ...
click
kapow!
NOT EVEN BATTLING SWARMS OF ALIENS ALONE ...
BUT NOW THAT HIS ONLY FRIENDS ARE IN GRAVE DANGER ...
squeak squeak
sploodge
HE IS TERRIFIED.
vooosh!

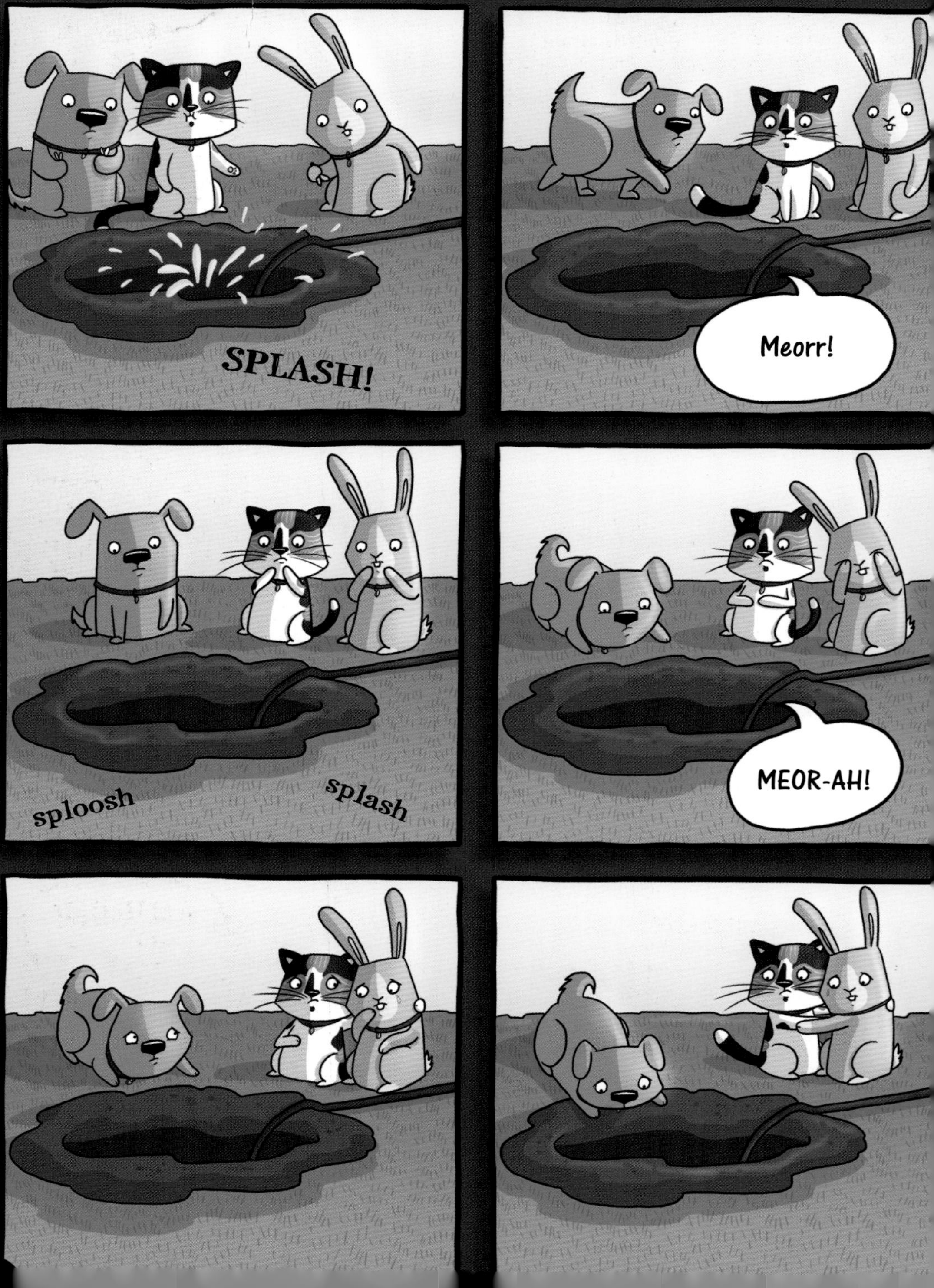
SPLASH!
Meorr!
sploosh
splash
MEOR-AH!

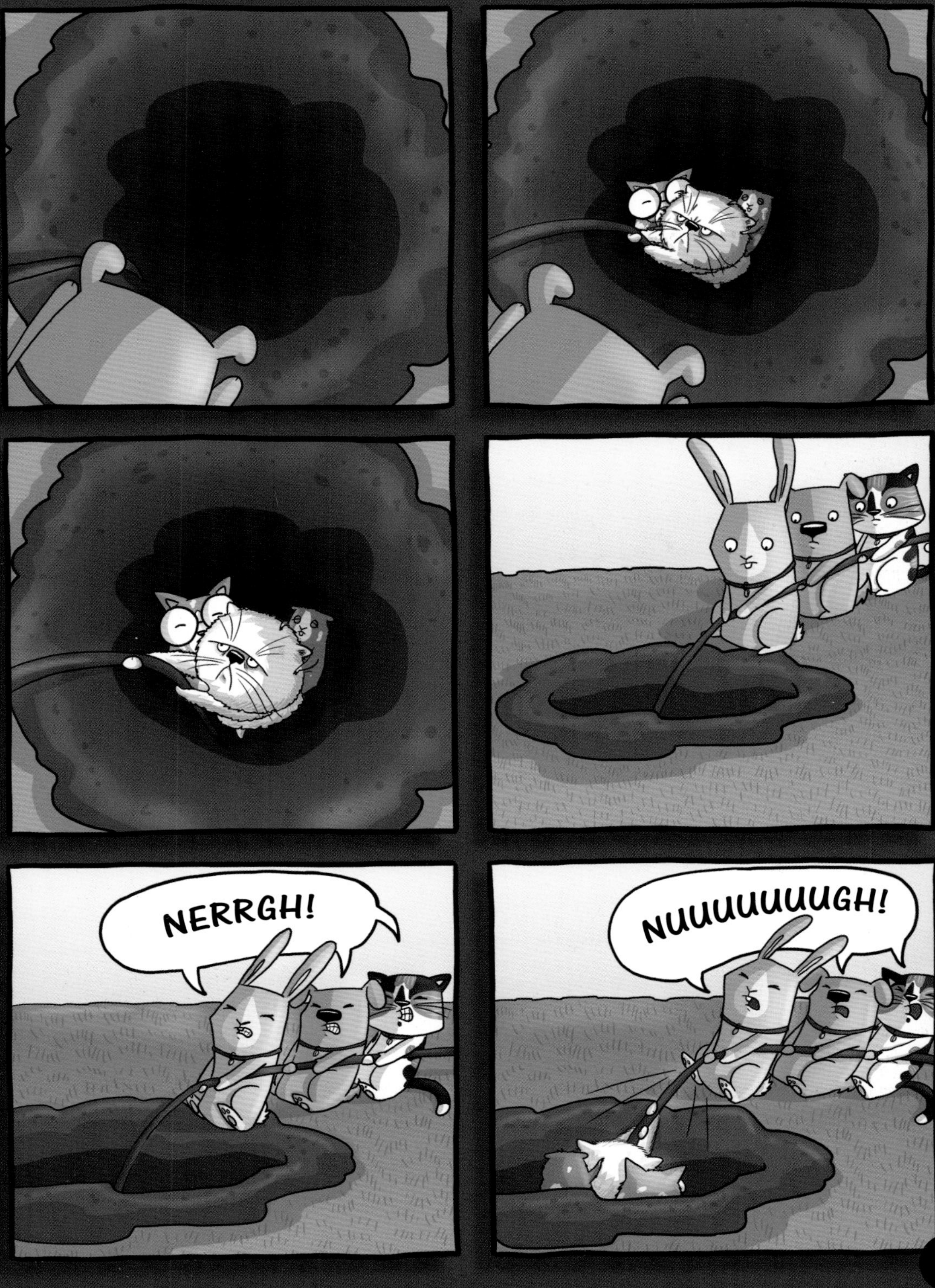
NERRGH!
NUUUUUUUUGH!

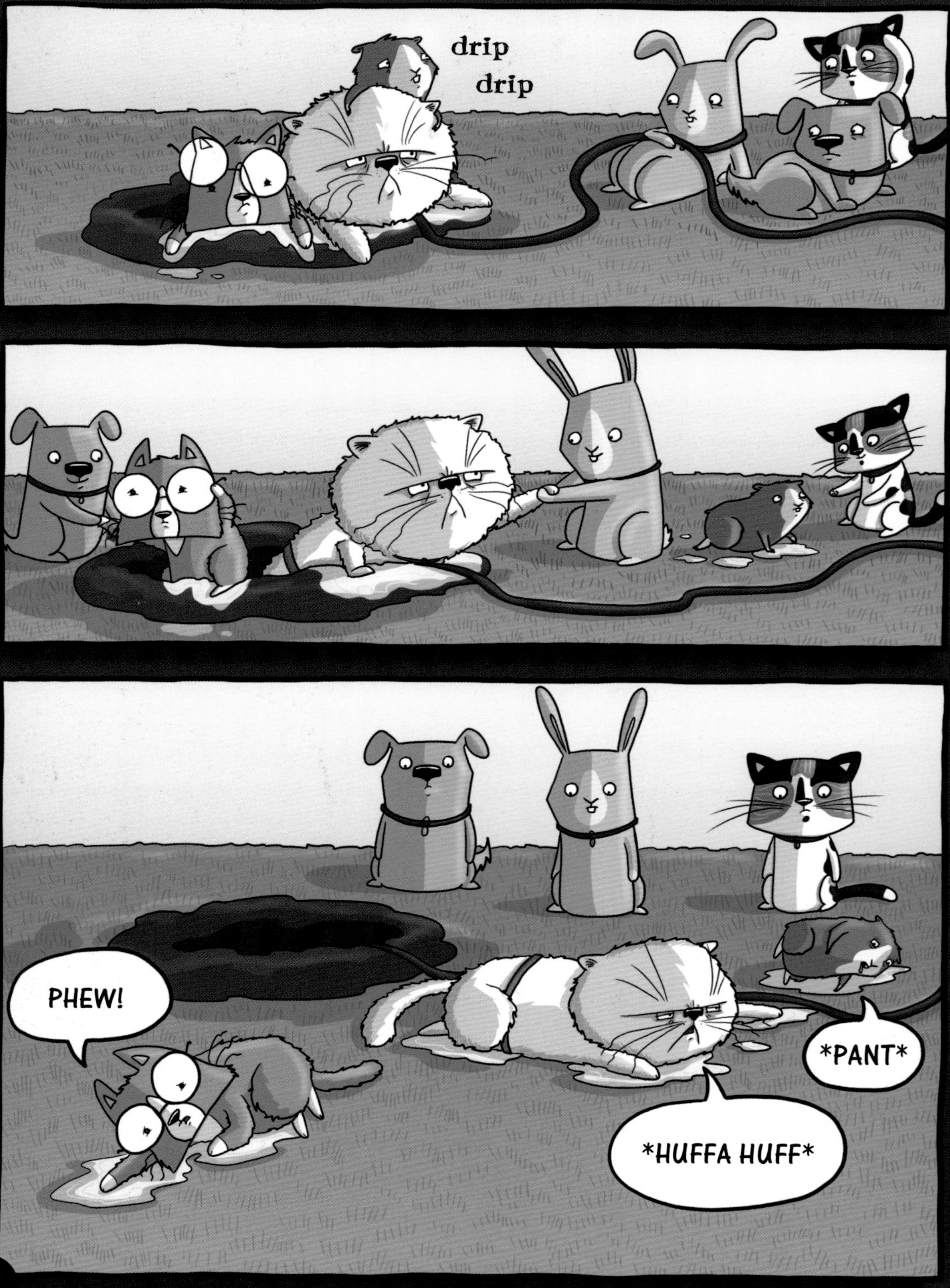

drip
drip
PHEW!
PANT
HUFFA HUFF

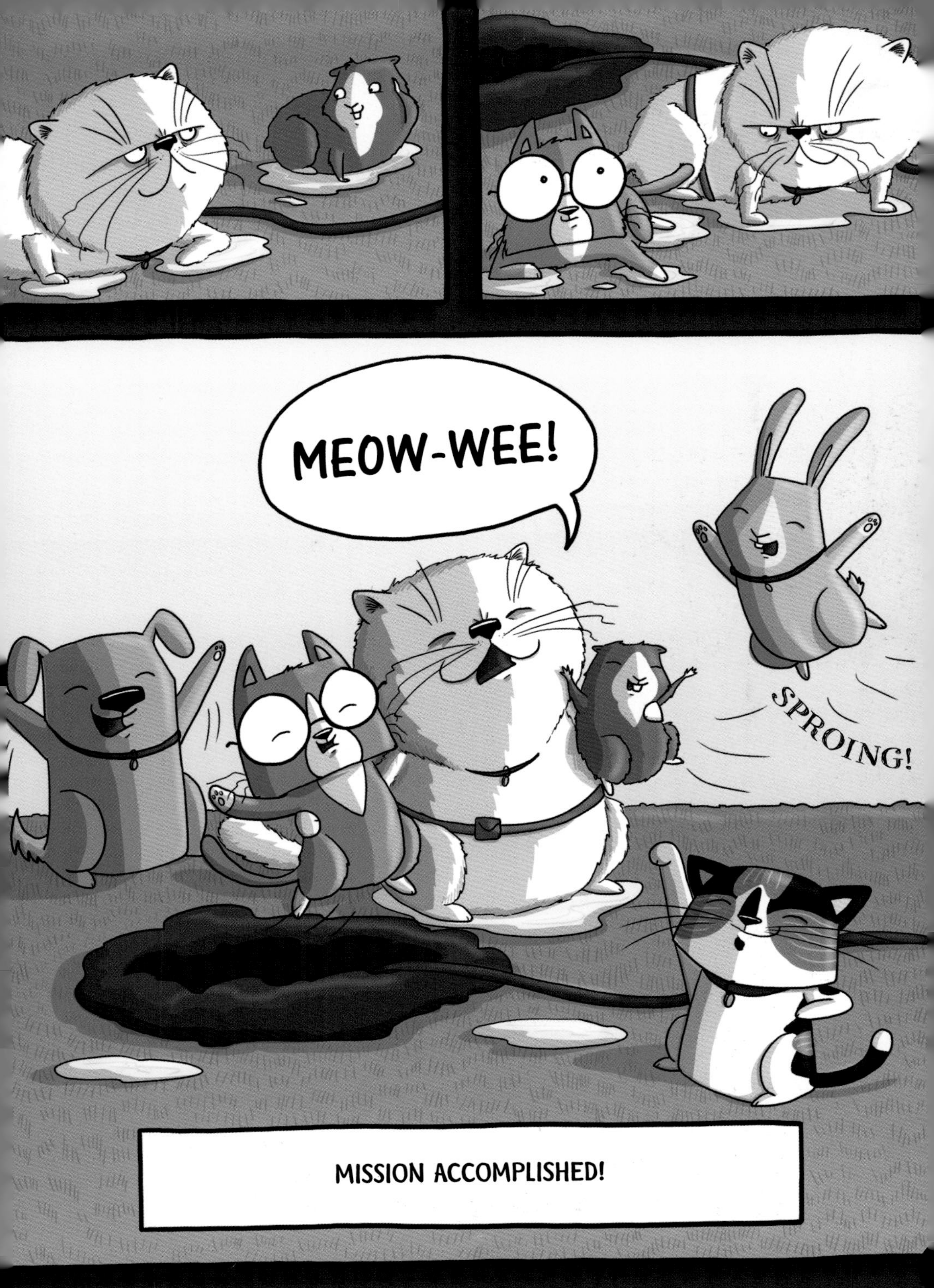
MEOW-WEE!
SPROING!
MISSION ACCOMPLISHED!

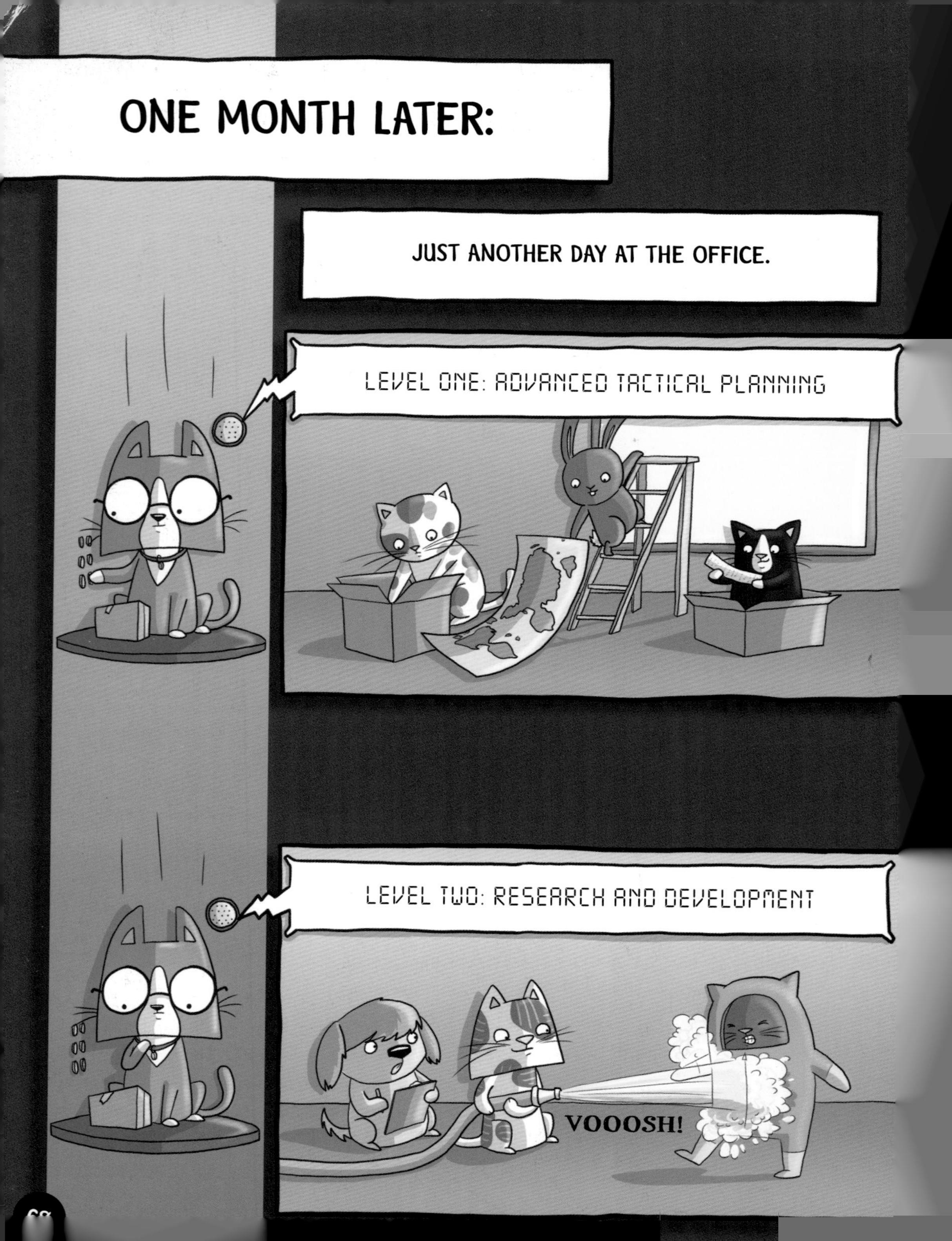
ONE MONTH LATER:
JUST ANOTHER DAY AT THE OFFICE.
LEVEL ONE: ADVANCED TACTICAL PLANNING
LEVEL TWO: RESEARCH AND DEVELOPMENT
VOOOSH!

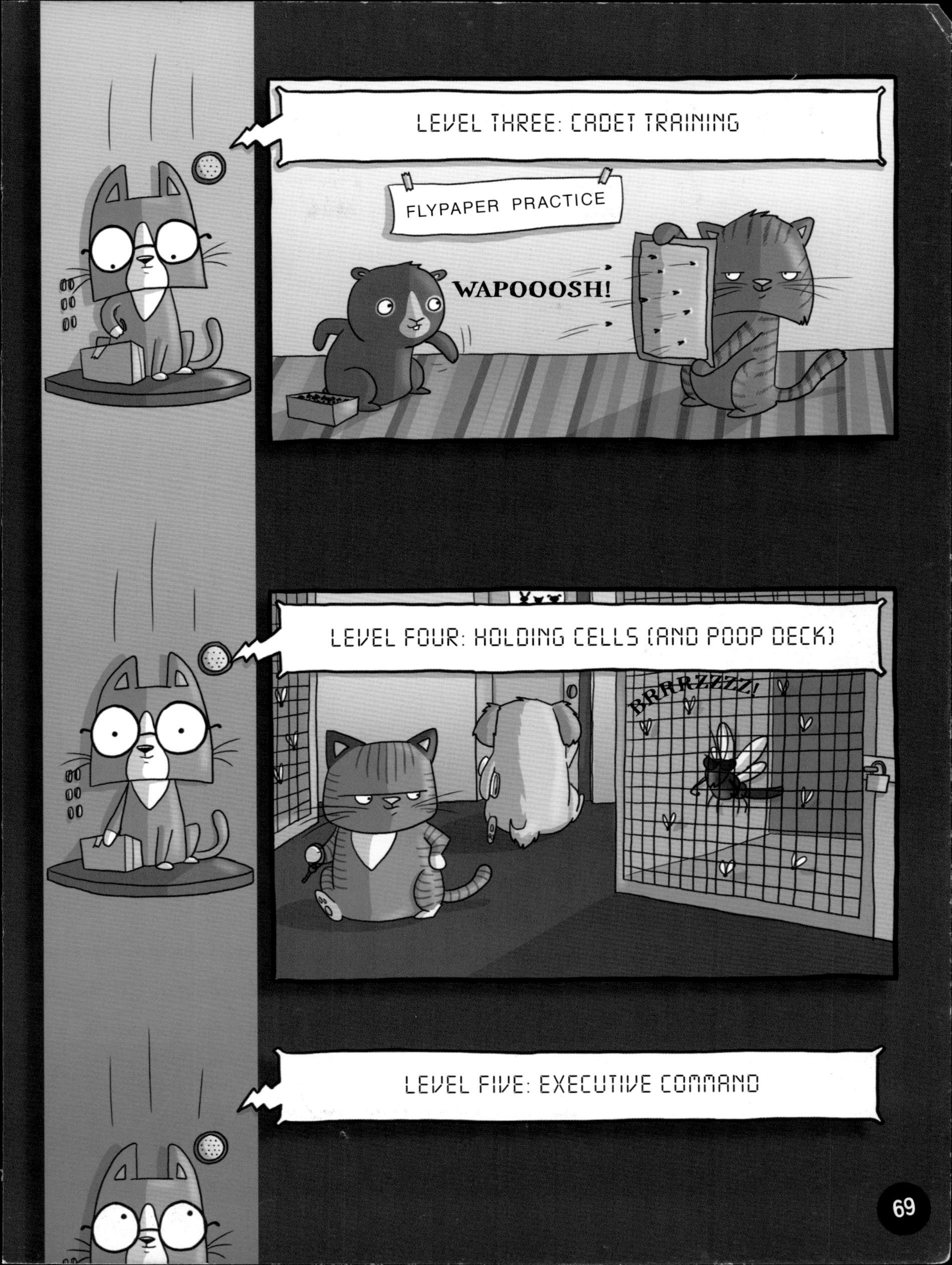
LEVEL THREE: CADET TRAINING
FLYPAPER PRACTICE
WAPOOOSH!
LEVEL FOUR: HOLDING CELLS (AND POOP DECK)
BRRRZZZZ!
LEVEL FIVE: EXECUTIVE COMMAND

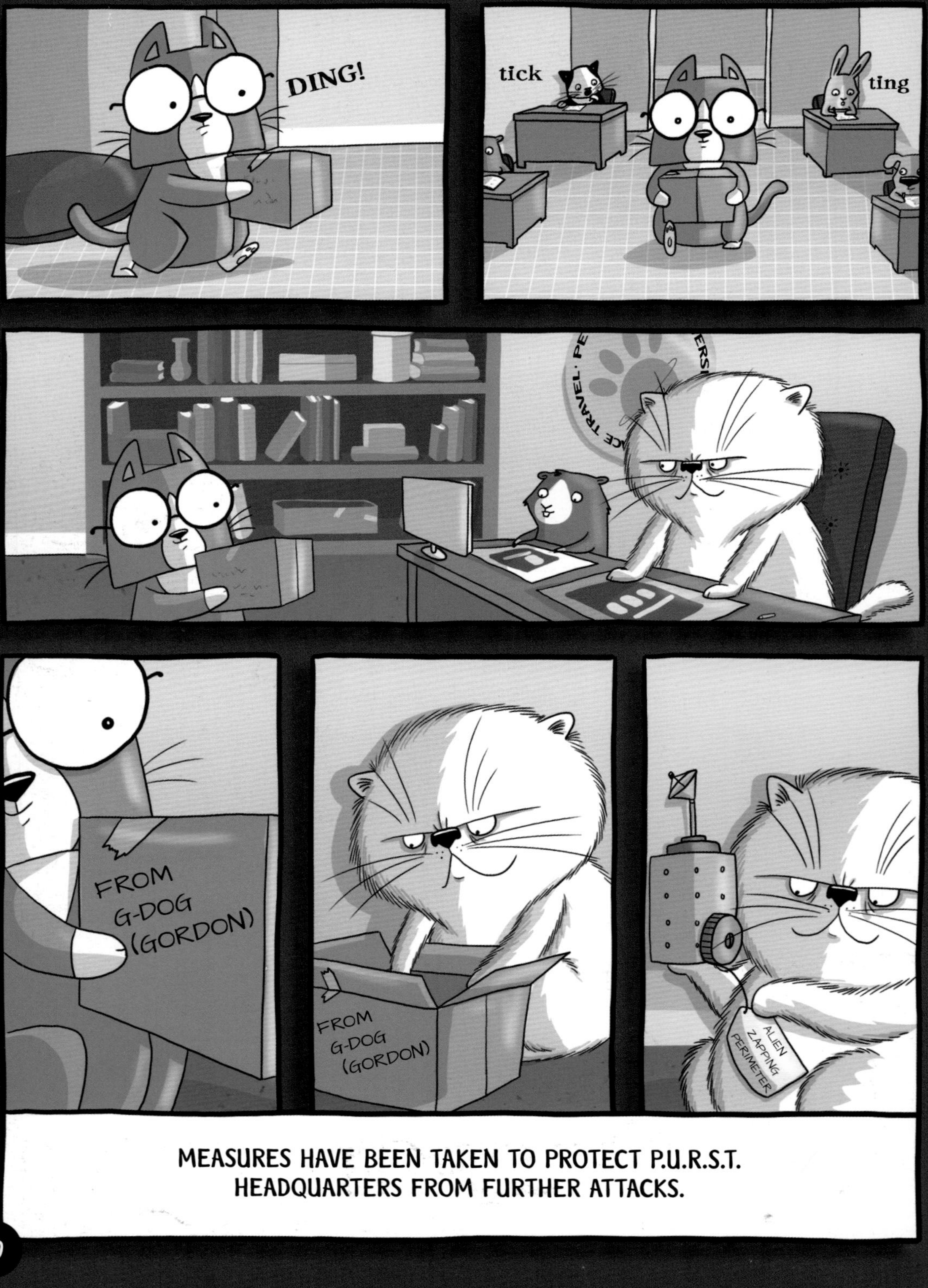
DING!
tick
ting
FROM G-DOG (GORDON)
FROM G-DOG (GORDON)
ALIEN ZAPPING PERIMETER
MEASURES HAVE BEEN TAKEN TO PROTECT P.U.R.S.T. HEADQUARTERS FROM FURTHER ATTACKS.

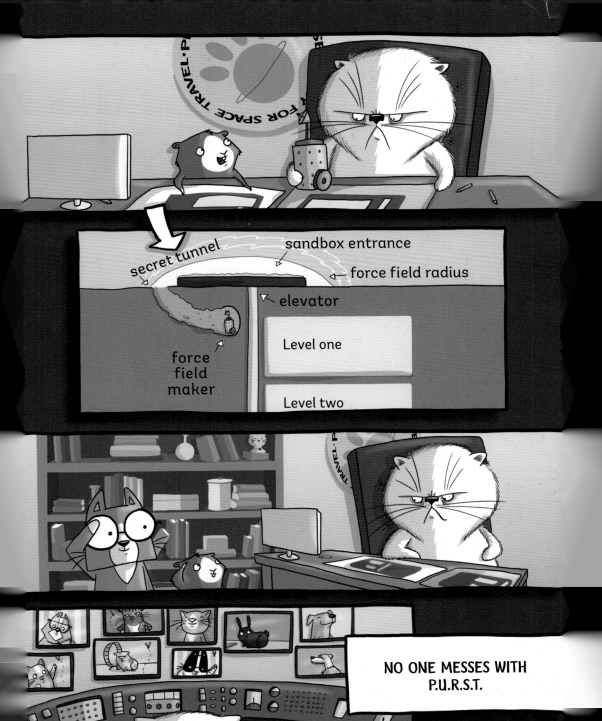

secret tunnel

sandbox entrance

force field radius

elevator

Level one

Level two

force field maker

NO ONE MESSES WITH
P.U.R.S.T.

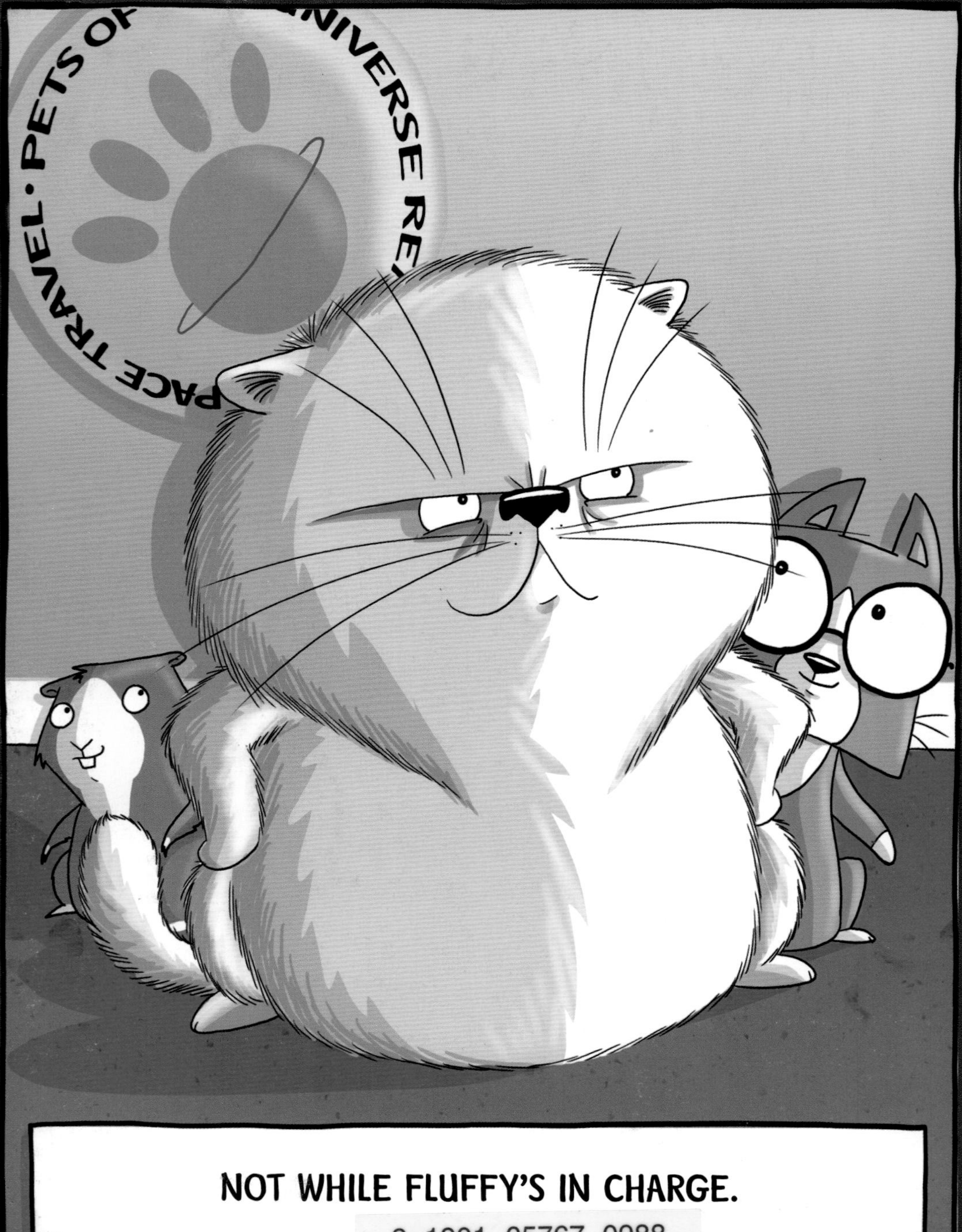
PETS OF THE UNIVERSE SPACE TRAVEL
NOT WHILE FLUFFY'S IN CHARGE.